BEFORE I AM ERASED

THE KEYHOLE CHRONICLES
BOOK 2

CHERIL N. CLARKE

GET A FREE BONUS CHAPTER

Join my newsletter to instantly get the first chapter of my next book (you will NOT regret it!): https://dl.bookfunnel.com/hkygıcy64a

1

THE THIRD CUP

PRESENT DAY: MIAMI, EARLY SPRING

Some mornings, the only way to keep from unraveling is to make something beautiful. And today, I had two ceremonies to prepare for. Sunlight slid over my hands as I arranged hibiscus in a blue ceramic vase. They'd wilt by afternoon, but I needed the color now. I craved something bright before the day had a chance to fade. A spirited grackle squawked from a nearby utility wire—the bird was loud and arrogant like it owned the block. But I smiled. Not even annoyed at the little fellow's shriek.

I had been awake since four-thirty because sleep abandoned me years ago. It was one of Ethiopia's parting gifts that had lasted decades. Meanwhile, my neighbors in this modest corner of Coconut Grove still slept as I transformed my apartment into a memory of home.

"I wonder why I don't just buy the pre-mixed spices from Publix," I mumbled to the empty kitchen, tapping a wooden spoon against the pot. Then I remembered I made a life of refusing shortcuts and rejecting style over substance.

A yawn curled itself out of me as my fingers worked. As if the mere mention of rest were enough to taunt me when I moved on to crushing cardamom pods. Their perfumed release made me smile, though, and my berbere simmered in clarified butter.

Fresh injera waited nearby under a cotton cloth. It was delivered at dawn by a bleary-eyed but dutiful youngster. "Selam, Dr. Bekele," he'd greeted, accepting my tip with a nod full of respect.

My kitchen counter displayed twenty-seven years of adaptation: Ethiopian spices in American measuring cups. An Italian espresso machine beside an old photo of me enjoying cherry blossoms in Washington, DC. The whole space was a design born from displacement.

"Hmph." I paused at a small mirror hung deliberately at eye level—a woman's face looked back. *My* face, lined yes, but still familiar and unchanged since the revolution. "So many lives tangled into one," I whispered before adjusting my netela to let the gold fabric cascade over one shoulder. A slight tremor in my left hand registered as I pinned it.

Just yesterday, the sales associate at a boutique called me "adorable" and "courageous" for choosing a dress with a waistline, as if my body should have retired along with my 401(k). *Eshi!* I'd exclaimed under my breath. My native tongue always slipped back when insults came gift-wrapped as compliments. I could only hope that I hadn't made such comments when I was younger. Perhaps I did out of naïveté, but now I recognize that tone as the same one I'd use to praise a toddler for wearing mismatched socks. Patronizing. And...regrettable.

Living long doesn't make you wise by default, but it does give you receipts. I've got years of them, tucked into memory and margins. And with enough time, I've learned what to return, what to throw out, and what to finally own.

I turned off the water and a few soapy suds hit my wrist. *Retired.* The word sounded really good. It sounded beautifully final, but if I were honest, it never quite stuck. Sometimes I missed the rigor of my work in forensic linguistics— listening for lies tucked inside language, tracking silence as carefully as speech. It was work made for women like me: precise, patient, and not easily fooled. But I didn't miss it enough to go back into the field full-time.

"Sixty-four years," I told the spices, the kitchen walls, and the ghosts of those who hadn't escaped. "We survived on this Earth. Sixty-four dynamic years."

But today was about the present, not the past.

THE DOORBELL soon chimed with the arrival of my guests— on time, which meant they were rushing. Africans understood time differently, but these women had been in America long enough to learn compliance.

"Alright, alright!" I grinned as I let them in. They were such a highlight.

A burst of color and heat entered, three wildfires in human skin. And not one of them apologized for what they'd burned away or the new growth they'd fed. Neither did I.

"Makeda!" Cheek kisses and warm greetings from all took hold.

All near my age and draped in traditional dress yet brightened even more with Miami's particular flamboyance, my friends swept in seconds apart. Almaz carried purple orchids. Seble brought honey wine. Yemi, always practical, held a bag of coffee beans superior to mine.

"You started without us," Almaz accused, giving me an extra squeeze in our hug.

"I woke with the birds," I replied, accepting their offerings with both hands—the proper way.

"Birds don't wake at four," Seble countered. "Only young mothers and women too old to pretend they sleep through the night."

My sanctuary didn't stand a chance. Within minutes, it burst into controlled chaos. Voices overlapped. Silk sleeves brushed counters. And shoes were kicked off in corners like it was their house, not mine. Between the trio's bare feet padding over my tile, I spotted a fresh henna pattern adorning one of their ankles. Almaz. She always wore her skin like an unapologetic art gallery.

Seble marched to the kitchen and shifted my incense burner three inches left. Tall, stern, still able to intimidate waiters with a glance, she said, "Makeda, this was crooked," and set down the bottle she'd brought.

They all preferred calling me my given name versus the "Mae" that I'd become over time.

"Ma'am, that was intentional!" I teased. "For aesthetic balance."

Almaz sniffed my coffee beans and clicked her tongue.

Theatrics in gold bangles, she asked, "Did you buy these from that boy with the lazy eye again?"

"He's sixteen and entrepreneurial. Be nice," I chuckled.

"Yemi, save her from herself," Almaz called.

"Yemi!" I echoed, grinning. "Tell her to stop insulting my beans and pour the wine."

Yemi was the friend who was soft-spoken until she wasn't. "Ha!" Was all she could offer before taking the glass to her lips.

It was a beautiful morning. Worldly jazz soon filtered in as someone adjusted a speaker volume. An artist's vibraphone filled the space like a second conversation. My kitchen had been hijacked. My senses were delighted. The women I trusted most had resumed their old dance: arguing, correcting, stirring, and laughing. I loved them for it.

"Too much salt in the berbere," Almaz announced from the stove.

"Not enough," Seble continued, tasting it straight from the spoon.

I clapped my hands once. It was loud enough to make them all pause. "Back away from the pot. This is a get together, not a coup."

That got a laugh.

Soon, we moved to the balcony for our regular coffee ceremony. A shiny jebena already sat at the center of the low table and fresh beans crackled over charcoal. The aroma bloomed as my friend's voice rose and fell like music. Their silver hair shone under the morning light while a mild breeze tugged their spice-colored scarves loose at their shoulders.

This gathering was a sisterly habit, even though none of us were blood-related. It was our bond. Our anchor. Our language and our chosen family get-together. They knew where to sit, which sugar cubes to pass, and when to fall quiet as I stirred the beans over the flame. We had all found each other in the second half of our lives and never let go.

"Such a beautiful day today," Yemi peeked out at the bay.

"Mm hm. A nice breeze," added Almaz.

But I felt it. Their watching. Quiet glances when I lifted something with my left hand. The way Yemi offered to carry the tray without saying why. She opened her mouth like she might say something, then stopped. Almaz eventually handed me the sugar cubes without a word as the ritual drew closer. Seble cleared her throat once. They were making room for me.

"Let me pour first," I kept my voice light. "It's tradition."

What I didn't say was: *I need to know if I can still do this.*

They obliged, and I served the coffee.

The first cup was steady.

The second: clean.

The third—my fingers double-crossed me, and a hot splash bloomed dark on the white tablecloth.

"Ahh!" I huffed, but no one gasped. No one moved. They just watched and waited while I finished pouring and set the jebena down. Then, despite being frustrated, I finally raised my cup.

"Today." I was a bit nervous, but clear. "I received confirmation of Parkinson's disease. And I've decided I won't let it ruin my life, nor will I vanish quietly into some placid senior state."

All three of their faces collapsed into shock and sympathy. I continued before they could probe me with questions and pity.

"Though it's been many years since I've lived there, our homeland is still in my blood. And in Ethiopia, we honor certainty—even difficult certainty—with coffee and company. Now I can name the enemy."

"Makeda..." Almaz touched my hand with one of hers while covering her mouth with her other.

Confusion rippled, but they followed the tradition. We each raised our cups, and the ceremony continued as it had for a thousand years across the ocean. Only the context and location had changed. I'd never seen a toast of bewilderment until today, but respect carried it through.

At least I still have that.

Later, as my friends filed out with promises of support, prayers, and help "not letting this thing take over my life," a usually charming neighbor passed by and called from across the walkway.

"Hosting a prayer group?"

"No," I told him. "Just friends."

He nodded with a too-familiar smile. "Always nice to see the older generation keeping busy."

Oh, go away! I wanted to say. But I didn't respond. I just waited until he turned the corner, then closed my door and leaned against it. I was so grateful for my sister circle, but also very tired. Dozens of thoughts stampeded through my mind. Tears still threatened to fall from my whirlwind day, but I forced them back. There was no point in falling apart now. *Keep control,* I told myself and breathed through the fault line of emotions swirling inside me. I had to rest the quake.

I opened my eyes. My living room was quiet again, but everything felt slightly off. The incense had tapered. The music was gone, and a green sliver of enamel caught the light near the bookshelf. I ignored it for now, knowing I had one more moment to tend to.

I crossed to my small altar with photos of my darling parents, a leather-bound Amharic Bible, and a vial of soil from Addis Ababa. Heart palpitations and anxiety rocked me as I lit a small beeswax candle. It wasn't entirely from the Parkinson's announcement this time. Today actually marked two beginnings: my journey with the disease, and the ritual of memory I've repeated on this date for forty-seven years. The anniversary of my first disappearance.

I opened the small woven pouch from my altar. Its fabric was faded from much handling. Inside was a tattered scrap of white cotton, still faintly stained with indigo. I pressed it to my face and inhaled with closed eyes. Nothing remained of its original scent—no market dust, no incense, no fear-sweat. Just time.

"Whatever I can't forget," I murmured. "I must keep contained."

Not all memories are sacred. Some are burdens. Some are blades. And some people—well, forgetting them is survival. Perhaps there was justice in it. The cloth in my hands once formed part of a funeral shroud. Not for a corpse, but for a living woman who needed to become invisible. I exhaled at length, and my homeland rose around me just as vividly as if it were yesterday...

Addis Ababa, Ethiopia 1976 – The Funeral That Wasn't

My heartbeat drummed inside my throat. A fly landed on my eyelid. I didn't dare blink. Couldn't. Even breathing felt like betrayal, and beyond the market's racket, a child laughed —sharp, gleeful, oblivious. The kind of sound that didn't know it was echoing over a grave. Sweat cooled too fast against my spine, and the smell of stale garlic and something rotting under a crate turned my stomach. I told myself the rot wasn't blood.

The first time I lied to America, I was mourning people who were still alive while trying not to join them. A funeral veil scratched against my neck as I crouched behind a stack of empty fruit crates in a Merkato. I could still feel the fabric pulling tightly against my torso. White is for mourning in Ethiopia, but that day, it was also for invisibility. Soldiers didn't look twice at grieving women. Grief made them uncomfortable; discomfort made them careless. I took advantage of that.

Through wooden slats, I watched three uniformed men questioning a produce vendor about university students, pamphlets, and meetings. The seller's eyes flicked briefly toward my hiding place before he shook his head.

"Allah witness, I sell only vegetables, not politics." He

motioned *no* while speaking. No, he did not know anyone they were after for being too vocal against the regime. What a beautiful lie. I was grateful.

My fingertips were stained indigo-blue from a mimeograph machine we operated all night in a professor's basement. The two thousand pamphlets we printed were then hidden beneath food crates in market stalls across Addis. By that evening, they would reach university dormitories, telling the truth about those who had vanished.

I could still remember the acidic sting of lemon when I wiped the papercuts on my fingers. It was a necessary burn. Back then, students who were too loud, too demanding, and too honest against power vanished overnight. Professors, too. Names were erased, and families were warned not to ask what happened to their daughters and sons, not to question why no one answered their letters. And if they did ask, someone came. We didn't say the name of the man who gave the orders, but we all knew who it was. His shadow touched everything.

In my canvas bag were three fake university ID cards, including new photos and new names for classmates who had to escape Ethiopia that night. I was young then—barely 21—but old enough to know which lies could save a life. Ever-charming, I'd found a bribable government clerk and I became the courier between fear and freedom.

The soldier stepped closer to my hiding place and my heart charged in my chest. Sweat ran down my back and the space between my breasts. I gulped before beginning the ritualized keening of a woman in mourning, rocking slightly, my face pressed to my knees.

"No, no, nooooo," I wailed.

"Who died?" he demanded, rifle barrel pushing aside a crate.

I looked up with giant tears. "My parents," I lied. "The fever took them."

His face twisted with superstition. *Death might be contagious*, I imagined him thinking. He stepped back.

"Go home, woman! The markets are no place for mourning."

I nodded and gathered my covering around me, clutching my bag of forged identities. The cold blade of a last-resort knife bit into my waistband. Thank God I never had to use it. "May God protect you," I whispered. Another untruth. I wouldn't feel a thing if the soldier died. It would have been a gift, in fact. God had truly vulnerable people to help.

When the gunner moved on, I counted to one hundred in Amharic before standing, still hunched in grief. Very theatrical. I then moved toward the university where three students waited for the papers to help them vanish from government lists.

"Keep walking!" a merchant hissed as I passed his stall. He didn't even look up from his scales. "They are watching the north gate now."

My legs pressed forward.

I had no way of knowing then that four years later, I too would disappear—into America, into marriage, into motherhood. That my future son would one day perfect the vanishing act I inadvertently taught him by example.

2

THE BOX
PRESENT DAY: MIAMI

The carved box on the bookshelf hadn't been opened in years. I'd deliberately placed it between two volumes I rarely needed and a broken incense burner I couldn't bring myself to throw away. For the most part, the old box behaved. Decorative. Dignified. Quiet.

Until tonight.

It leaned forward, not quite fallen, but still askew. It begged me to take notice.

"Everything finds its way out of place these days." I grumbled while climbing a stepstool.

Two nights had passed since the ceremony and my diagnosis reveal. Two days since I'd spilled coffee onto the tablecloth and called it a toast. My friends had gone home, and I'd spent the last two days pretending I wasn't waiting for something to arrive. A harsher symptom, maybe...or clarity. Even grief. Anything.

But tonight, it was the box.

The once hand-painted wood felt ancient but familiar. When I tried the latch, it didn't budge. Still, I brushed the dust from its faded cover, and pressed harder. Again, nothing. My fingers—stiff and less obedient now—couldn't find the precise angle and pressure I remembered. The mechanism hadn't changed. I had. Damn it.

I tried again but my thumb slipped. My hand trembled even more than I meant it to.

"Forget it," I muttered, stepping down slowly.

I stared at the vintage chest from below. The last time I'd opened it, I was still working a traditional job. I was less weak and off-balance. Still sharp. Less clumsy... I was still capable of forgetting things on purpose. But here I am not even remembering how to open it, or what I'd put inside the damn thing. And now, that memory gap felt dangerous. I hated not knowing. But I hated asking for help more. Regardless, I picked up the phone and dialed.

"Good evening. I need someone to open something," I said, when the locksmith answered. The call was quick and solution-oriented.

"I can be there tonight," the owner-operator offered.

He arrived later—just after six—and was polite enough not to knock twice. I liked that. Men who knocked more than once were usually the same ones who'd keep calling after goodbye. And I couldn't stand that.

The door opened to a gentleman who was leaner than his voice had suggested. His long frame and sinewy posture caught me off guard. "Hello," I greeted, noting his blue work shirt with rolled sleeves and well-worn jeans. His boots had clearly seen lots of tile, concrete, and marble.

"Good evening, I'm Ezra from Unlock the Grove." His eyes flicked across my face, then down. Subtle. Not rude. Ezra took inventory the way someone does when they're used to entering private spaces. "Mae Bekele?"

I nodded. "Thank you for coming."

"It's my pleasure, ma'am." He gave a slight and professional smile, highlighting his gray beard. "You said it was a carved box that was stuck?" Ezra felt a few years younger than me, but like he could pass for even younger due to his nice physique.

"Yes. It's this way," I said, stepping aside.

He paused at the threshold, clocking my bare feet on the tile—brown, a little wide, and strong. Then he removed his boots without being asked. My brows furrowed. *He definitely pays attention.* Ezra wasn't the cheapest option, but I'd read enough of his online reviews to know he handled antiques and restoration work very well.

"Nice place," he offered, while following me with polite chatter.

"Thank you. It's honest," I answered.

That usually ended small talk. It didn't.

"Have you been in Miami long?" Ezra eyeballed a cracked photo frame on my bookshelf.

"Twenty years. Before that, D.C. And Addis before that."

"Long way from North Florida. That's where I'm from." He paused. "Addis?"

"Ethiopia."

"Wow! I've always wondered about Africa. Never did get the chance to visit the continent." Ezra glanced toward a wall of hardcovers. "Looks like you read for a living."

My lips pursed and I raised my eyebrows, but he couldn't see my expression from behind. We reached the table, and he barely stopped talking. The carved box sat at the center.

"It used to open easily, but now it's behaving like a vault."

"Do you remember when it was made? It's a beautiful piece."

"Thank you! And I wish I did."

"No problem. I'll get it open for you." Ezra crouched and studied it. He unrolled a bag of tools. "An older piece like this usually means a handmade lock with no standard parts. You've got to listen to it a little."

I didn't respond, but I stayed upright.

"Sometimes they seize up from dust. Sometimes from memory."

Such an unexpected statement. "That's poetic."

"Unintentionally," he responded. "I work alone too much. Makes a man start narrating things." He pressed lightly on one corner. The box didn't move. "Might be a second mechanism. Some of these vintage ones were made in layers, especially if they were custom."

"I did have a compartment added years ago. I thought it might be useful, and then I forgot what was in there."

He turned slightly toward me.

"You forgot what's inside?"

"I forgot it mattered."

He grunted and shrugged. "Alright."

The silence between us lasted only a moment.

"I can see this one just isn't ordinary."

"Ha! Nothing in my life ever is," I quipped.

"Honestly, ma'am, I'll need to come back tomorrow with

a specialized tool to access the third compartment properly. If that's alright with you?"

"Yes, that would be fine. What time?"

"Does eight work for ya?"

"Yes, it does." I nodded, suddenly conscious of my slumped posture and trembling hand. I straightened up and closed my fingers into a small fist before he could notice. Ezra packed his tools quietly. I found myself watching his hands instead of my own. He didn't look at me again until the kit was closed.

"Thank you," I declared as he stood to leave. "For coming on short notice and your care with my things."

"It's part of the job, ma'am." He flashed a warm smile that revealed a single dimple I hadn't noticed earlier. "Locks are personal. Whatever's inside them, even more so."

"Mm hm."

"I talk too much when I work," he confessed bashfully. He only needed one more step to be outside of my door. "My old mentor blamed nerves. I think it's just habit." Then, glancing at the box: "If it starts talking while I'm gone, don't answer it!"

"Goodnight, Ezra," I held the smile just long enough to guide him out then chuckled in bewilderment. He had a kind energy about him that oddly made me feel uneasy instead of not. "I'll see you tomorrow at eight." Still, I appreciated him in my space.

I exhaled and rubbed my forehead the moment the door clicked shut. Quite the character he was. Plus... it had been a *long day*. My cell phone again stared at me next. A series of buzzes from incoming texts were waiting for me. A group chat with Almaz, Seble, and Yemi lit up with photos of a turquoise-painted house and sweeping ocean views.

"What is this all about?" I wondered aloud.

Almaz: *I just booked this for next month. 4 days. No arguments. It's been too long since we've taken a trip!*

Seble: *Doctor approved. Fresh air is medicinal, especially in Key West!*

Yemi: *Oh, I love this!! Don't worry, I'll handle the food!*

I stared at the images, a stunning Florida sunset reflected off windows in a place I had not imagined myself any time soon. But the pull of adventure and ocean views was already drawing me. A road trip with the girls used to be an annual thing, but the last few years something had always gotten in the way of us going anywhere.

"This is no time to travel," I tried convincing myself. "My health and everything..." the words were nasty on my lips. Inauthentic.

I *wanted* to go. And Almaz was right. It had been too long. I clutched my cell, and my thumb hovered over the keyboard before I typed: *What should I pack?*

Three dots appeared immediately from all of them. I smiled and set the phone down. I stayed in my chair, letting the silence stretch. Somewhere in the group chat, they were surely debating swimsuits and sun hats like it was 1998. I used to plan our trips. I used to lead. But somewhere along the way, I let go of more than I meant to.

Maybe the exhaustion of always being at the helm got to me. Of all the task lists that never seemed to end when in any form of leadership. Maybe it was easier to shrink than take up space after a while. But that wasn't the real me. The real me once loved just as hard as she rebelled. She used to dance barefoot in the rain and sometimes trusted too easily. She survived regimes, borders, triumphs, consequences...and the kind of silence that swallows people whole. But...perhaps I had gotten tired of making some people uncomfortable just by existing. Yet even when my own son erased me, I didn't vanish, I adapted. Women like me always do.

Alex hadn't spoken to me in nearly fifteen years. Not since his final college days. Not in any meaningful way, at least. None of my friends had ever met him. He eventually told people I was dead and leaned completely into surface-level visuals of perfection and success. Clean edges. No mess. Certainly not including a mother with a history like mine. And he never forgave me for moving him from DC to Miami when his father and I divorced. I still hurt from that.

The reality of my life pressed tightly against my heart in that lonely moment. Everything. The distance from my son. The way the world forgets women like me. The way the body slowly becomes less and less able to do what it once did with ease. *Sigh.* But I wasn't done yet. Not with my mind. Not with my voice. Not with the truth. And thank God, I was not alone either. Far from it. I had the most dynamic, courageous, loud and loving sister circle.

In that moment, I realized I didn't want to undo the past. I wanted to reclaim the version of myself the world forgot: bold, full of conviction—and FUN! I wanted to speak the truths I buried and write the story no one ever asked me for. Not for history or for vanity, but for my soul. And maybe for the son who stopped calling.

3

THE RECORDING

It was already warm out before the sun fully came up. Salt from the bay wafted through the air as I took my time with an early morning walk. A sanitation worker swept leaves into a plastic dustpan near the curb.

"Beautiful morning," he coaxed while glancing up.

"Depends on your definition of beautiful," I countered.

That made him chuckle. "Fair enough."

I kept walking, telling myself to have less snark. Less bite. I didn't have to be a flirt, but I could have been more...generous. After I passed the man with the broom, I kept walking for a few more blocks before slowing down—just to see if my body could still handle it. It could.

I checked behind me only to see early shadows and swaying trees. In that moment, I slipped my phone from my pocket, swiped down to the voice recorder app and tapped the red, circular button.

"I've never said this out loud," I began. "Not to Almaz. Not to my ex-husband or son."

I paused. Afraid to death but knowing I needed to get the truth out. I could not stifle it any longer. My shoes scuffed against the pavement.

"When I left Ethiopia..." I exhaled heavily. "I wasn't alone." I gulped. "I was pregnant. Barely. I lost it somewhere over the Atlantic, in a bathroom on the plane. Told the flight attendant I had food poisoning. I never spoke of it again."

My voice wavered, yet I didn't stop.

"It wasn't Alex. He came later. This was something else. Someone else. And I buried her before she had a name."

I closed my eyes. The sun pressed against my face like it was trying to decide whether to warm or expose me.

"If I die and no one knows that... I don't know. Maybe I just didn't want to be the only one who remembered."

I saved the file and titled it "What I Never Said," but without playing it back. It was just the truth, spilling out in a way that I'd organize later somehow. The words scraped their way out. My throat burned. My chest felt raw. Both of my forearms shook from the release. I had not spoken that truth aloud in over forty-five years. A part of me wanted to buckle, but I stood still instead. It was like I'd torn open an old wound that had healed dirty but held anyway. Step one: getting it all out. Step two: staying upright long enough to face what came next.

It was time to go home.

By seven o'clock, the heat already pressed through my lightweight cotton dress as I made my way through palm tree flanked streets. I smiled more this time. Waved at a few people. And boosted my mood through being more *active*. But in a snap, I halted. Instead of rushing home to prep for Ezra, I texted him to ask if he could come at noon instead. I wanted to go to my doctor first. If I didn't stop by the clinic now, I might talk myself out of facing my new reality head-on.

"How about one o'clock?" Ezra countered.

"That's fine. I'm sorry for the last-minute change."

"It's no problem at all. I'll see you then," he obliged.

I was just passing my building when I ended the call and heard, "Back already, Ms. Mae?" from the security guard.

"Not just yet. Going to make one more stop." I smiled back in earnest.

Kelvin grinned and nodded. His youthful face was framed by a neatly shaped beard and the kind of smooth skin that hadn't learned to worry yet. "Take your time. It's such a nice day out."

"Indeed it is!" I kept on walking.

THE CLINICAL WAITING room was too cold. Almost frigid. Surely, it didn't need to be this icy to kill whatever germs might be in the air.

I sat near a window under dishonest sunlight that didn't warm anything. Across from me, a child tapped the side of an orange juice box without drinking. His mother scrolled her phone without blinking.

A poster above the receptionist's desk caught my eye with its smiling cartoon neurons speaking in cheerful speech bubbles. One read, *"I fire, therefore I am."* Nerdy me almost laughed, but my nerves held me back. Soon enough, a nurse finally called my name. She didn't ask how I was. Just confirmed my date of birth and told me to follow. I did.

The hallway walls were pale green with scuffed baseboards, and every third ceiling tile was a different shade of white. I passed two open doors—one with a patient fussing about needles, the other with an empty scale in the middle of the room.

"Here we are!" she announced.

We entered Exam 3, where there was a chair, stool, and counter with no music or pretense. I didn't like this place. I didn't recall it feeling so emotionless the last time I was there.

"Dr. Greene will be in shortly." The nurse advised, halfway out the door. "I'll be in and out to check on you. Please have a seat," she pushed out a half-smile. *Maybe she was just having a bad day*, I thought, giving her the benefit of the doubt.

I rested on the paper-covered table with my hands folded in my lap. Fidgeting. Thinking.

"Dr. Bekele," Dr. Greene greeted. He was young and polite. No coat today—just a button-up shirt and a tablet he didn't look up from for the first few seconds.

"I read your chart." He lifted his eyes to meet mine. We relaxed into small talk before he said, "We're seeing some progression."

Dr. Greene softened the word, but it still hung.

"How much?" I could feel my body slumping but willed it to stay upright. "And, please, call me Mae."

The doctor tapped. He scrolled. "More tremor frequency and fine motor delays are showing up in your left hand. Possibly some speech disruption emerging. It's too early to call, but not too early to plan, Mae." He rested his hand on the table near me.

I inhaled, nodded, and exhaled.

"I'd like us to start speech therapy now. Also, occupational. It won't reverse anything, but it can help you hold the line a while longer." He slid a brochure toward me.

I glanced at it and frowned at the muted colors, staged photos of smiling women balancing yoga balls. *I don't want that,* I thought.

"Any questions?" Dr. Greene probed.

"No...not yet."

My answer must have satisfied him because he immediately stood. "If you agree to starting therapy, please call. Don't wait."

"Promise I will."

"Alrighty! I hope to hear from you soon." The door closed behind him with a quiet click.

Healthcare was lacking. I didn't feel cared for. I felt like a number. And though I hated to admit it, I *was* afraid. This was another valley of life that I seemed to be coasting down faster than I'd even realized I was journeying. *Progression.* The word hurt, but I was stronger than the pain. Experienced with it, too.

As the room hummed with air vents and ghost voices from the hallway, I shifted on the clinical paper draping the table beneath me. "It is what it is," I mumbled, and, eventually got up and went outside.

The South Florida sun hit me hard. It was so bright and too sudden. A bird somewhere made a sharp call and the shrill made me flinch.

"Just for one day," I said aloud. "I wish someone else could carry my name—any version of it from any time. Just for a day... so I can hear it without having to be the one answering to it." Step by cautious step, I made it to my car. My nerves were awful, and my skin was hot from angst.

I didn't cry. The urge came close, but I boxed it up neatly and tightly before starting my engine. When I got home, I turned on the kitchen light, then turned it back off. I flexed my fingers and my feet. Neck rolls with my left palm cupping the back of my collar.

Nothing felt right, and I hadn't eaten. I didn't want to. I needed something, though—tea, maybe—but even that required choosing a cup. I was tired of choosing! That's when the knock came.

"One o'clock already?" I couldn't believe the time had passed so quickly. I'd wanted to freshen up and throw on a different scarf and earrings, but it was too late.

I saw Ezra through the peephole. He stood exactly as I imagined he would: upright, unbothered, and not checking his phone.

"Apologies," I offered, when opening the door. My breath was caught between annoyance and dignity. "Time got away from me again."

"No trouble." His voice was forgiving. "I always give people grace."

"Do you now?" I pushed myself to *be* the kindness he offered.

"Maybe only the interesting ones." He winked. Ezra wore a dark gray shirt and the same worn boots. His eyebrows looked bushier in the daytime, and something citrusy clung to him. Ezra's energy was disarming.

"Please, come in."

Ezra stepped out of his shoes again without being asked. A leather bag was slung over his shoulder, and something metallic jostled quietly inside as he moved.

"May I get you something to drink?"

"Water's perfect, thank you."

I nodded and walked to the kitchen.

Ezra crouched near the table before I returned. I watched as he laid out his tools. His fingers moved with a certainty that made me both envious and respectful. I set the beverage down beside him and he gave a quiet thanks before reaching for a flat-headed probe.

"Have you always worked in this business?" I quizzed. I needed a distraction from the melee of health-related thoughts in my head.

"Actually, I have. Not always alone though."

"Oh?"

He hesitated. "It used to be me and my brother. We started together. He's more into high-end installations now. Secret drawers in kitchen floors. Safes hidden in bookcases. That kind of thing."

"And you prefer puzzles."

"I like quiet problems with clean solutions."

"It's a shame life rarely offers either."

"Which is why I stick to objects."

"You don't work with your brother anymore?" I paced.

"No. Not in a long time." Ezra didn't elaborate, and I didn't press.

The first click came low, mechanical, and satisfying.

"I'm going to pause here a second," he said. "Want to make sure the next layer doesn't bind." Ezra reached for another tool and wiped a smudge off the lid with the edge of his sleeve.

Just then, my phone buzzed on the counter. I checked the screen: *Almaz.* I stepped away to take the call, knowing these damn cell phones still allowed others to hear more than they should when it was at my ear.

"Makeda, did you eat anything yet? I'm nearby. We can grab a bite."

"Good afternoon." I chuckled. "Yes. I've eaten."

"Coffee isn't food."

"I'm not alone, Almaz."

I caught Ezra's hands slightly slowing though he didn't make a sound. He was listening.

"Call me later," I spoke more quietly, before disconnecting.

Ezra spoke next. "Trouble?"

"Old women with too much time and Wi-Fi."

He laughed out loud at that. "Heh! Those are the most dangerous kinds!"

The box gave a second click. This one deeper.

"There it is," he said proudly.

I watched him lift the lid slowly with both hands.

He looked up at me. "Do you want me to step away while you check it?"

"Stay," I told him, surprising even myself.

Inside was a photo of me in a crimson dress with big hair, big energy, and a big mouth. I was yelling something defiant into the crowd gathered at my old university. There were also a few old letters, a ring from my grandmother, and a black cassette tape with no label tucked between a folded scarf. "Hmph." I grunted. My hand momentarily became completely still, holding the photo. The past looked me in my face so boldly. So confidently. *Look at me...* It had been so many lifetimes ago since I was that young woman—barely twenty. I could feel my heart racing, too.

Ezra just stood there for a moment before gathering his things. "I'll send you a follow-up note about the mechanism," he told me. "That box could use a light oiling every few weeks to keep it from seizing again."

I quietly acknowledged while staring at the tape.

"Do you still have a player for that?" he quizzed.

"Probably somewhere."

He offered a small smile. "If not, I've got one at my shop. People bring in old stuff all the time. I'm happy to help you with it."

A silence.

I wasn't sure if I wanted to hear whatever the cassette held.

Ezra stepped toward the door. "Thanks for the water," he declared. "And the company."

"You were working, not socializing."

"True. But it didn't feel like work the whole time." He held my gaze. Ezra pulled a slim card from his back pocket. "You already have my info," he told me, placing it on the console near the door. "But this one's got the number that goes straight to me—not the dispatcher."

An uninvited smile immediately broke through. He clocked it and mirrored it blushingly. I looked at his card but didn't reach for it.

"If you find more boxes... or just... need something fixed..."

"Mm hm." I kept my voice noncommittal.

He smiled like he expected that. "Take care, Mae."

And he left. Only after the door clicked shut did I realize I was still standing there with the random items looked at me. I put Ezra's card in the desk drawer where I worked. Just in case.

I picked up the cassette tape and turned it over. It was sticky with old label residue. I wasn't ready to press play and get answers from it. Not yet. Instead, I traced my finger over the edge of the photo one more time.

"Look at my stance and my pride," I spoke aloud. "That woman with the roaring fire was still in me somewhere buried under layers of caretaking, departure, and the damp brush of memories."

The blaze was definitely still there. Dimmed maybe, but not out. The phone gave my heart an electric charge, and I loved it. I'd lived through too much to fade now. I grinned and closed the box quickly when my doorbell chimed. *Ding-dong!* A second ring immediately followed.

A look through the peephole revealed Almaz, impatient as always.

"One moment!" I called, sliding the box onto the highest

shelf of my bookcase. My hand juddered again, making me fumble. *Ding-dong!* The doorbell rang a third time.

Jesus Christ. I opened the entrance mid-ring. "I heard you the first time, woman."

"And I called you three times before that," Almaz countered. She breezed past me in a cloud of sandalwood and confidence. Her bracelets jangled as she set a glossy folder and bag of food on my counter. "You look...disturbed. What's happened?"

"Nothing." I smoothed nonexistent wrinkles from my dress. "A locksmith was just here."

Almaz's eyes narrowed slightly, following my gaze toward the bookshelf. "A locksmith? For what?"

"An old box. It's nothing."

"Nothing doesn't make your eyes look like that, Makeda." She studied me hard. Almaz had the kind of arms that could carry a watermelon and still wear bangles. I envied that fit physique now. "Whatever it is," she spoke again, "you can tell me later. First, look at this."

She opened the folder to reveal photos of a beach house with wide windows facing the ocean. Images of water excursions and delectable seafood platters were next. Shrimp. Crab. Lobster. Fish. It was mouth-watering.

I had not a moment to sulk over my health or history. "So, Key West," I leaned in to see clearer details of the property. I had to admit it was stunning. "You all are serious about this trip?"

"Did you think we weren't?" Almaz retrieved a shopping list from the folder. "Seble is handling transportation. Yemi's doing food. I've got activities and wardrobe. You just show up and enjoy life."

"Wardrobe?" I raised an eyebrow. This was a lot, and it was fast with everything else I had on my mind.

"Yes. Just coordinating for one of the dinners, you know... like we used to do."

She smiled and pushed the folder closer. "Four days. Sun. Ocean. No responsibilities. When was the last time you did something just because it felt *good*, Makeda? I know you have new things to think about but there's so much opportunity to balance it with more fun."

Her question landed harder than she probably intended. "It's been a while."

"Exactly." She squeezed my hand. "And whatever is in that box you're hiding, is something we can talk about another night." Almaz got up to leave and crossed the table. "Lord, I forgot to properly give you the dinner I picked up for you. Just heat it up a bit, huh, Makeda? You need to eat and keep up your strength."

"Almaz."

"Good night." She hugged and kissed me on the cheek and bolted towards the door. My friend was always so energetic.

After she left, I sat quietly for several minutes. Her words settled around me like dust. I must have soon dozed off because the next thing I knew it was late afternoon at Lake Langano—scores ago on the black shores of Ethiopia....

There I was, barefoot on warm sand. A young woman again. Music pulsed from somewhere out of view. Bright horns with a rhythm full of hips.

My cotton shawl caught wind and danced in front of the red ocean. Someone clapped in time. And I laughed so loud —and unbothered—before spinning, just to feel my linen skirt whip around my legs. Light dappled through palm trees and the air tasted of mango and smoke. *Home.*

"Yene konjo!" someone called out with a grin—that's right. A young woman with waist beads snapped her fingers. "Makedaaa," she crooned. "You still got it?"

Teenage me winked. *Always.* And then I dipped low to let my arms ride the music.

There was a blur of bodies around us. Sweating. Flirting. Happy. Carefree. No one was watching yet everyone was watching. I felt seen and untouched all at once. I even heard the honk and shrills of flamingos in the nearby national park. I loved the rawness of it all. But then there was static. It wasn't exactly sound but whatever the dream-state version of white noise or snow on a TV. The daylight dimmed and the music warped. A baritone voice called my name again this time. Not flirtatious. Just a single word, slow and flat. "Makeda."

I turned toward it but woke up instead. Back to the present. *Huh?*

My mouth was dry, and the sheets twisted at my ankles. The silence tasted like saltwater. I blinked, reaching for nothing. A laugh echoed in my head and I tried to fully come back to the present, and then I realized, the joy was mine. Wild and free. I smiled.

4

FILED UNDER MY NAME

Two days later, I found myself at The Miami Cultural Heritage Center. I'd hoped the place might have an old cassette player. It was the main reason I came. The building was tucked inside a former post office, standing confidently amid the glass-skinned condos and modern storefronts. I volunteered here occasionally, sorting through memories other people wanted to forget.

The Center preserved immigrant ephemera—letters, photos, textiles, bits of ritual, and language that didn't fit neatly into archives but meant everything to the people who carried them. It had stories from the Caribbean, Latin America, and Africa.

"Good morning!" A staffer greeted me.

I returned the hello and mentioned my request. Unfortunately, their tape player was broken. Disappointed but unwilling to waste the trip, I made my way to a workstation for a little solitude. But...I wasn't alone.

"Doc B! You're here!" A squeaky voice rang out, bright as a brass bell, and chewing gum the whole while.

Kai Jean stood by the archival scanner in a brilliant yellow jumpsuit. Multiple earrings adorning her ears caught the light—one being shaped like an old school boombox from the 2000s. Kai's braids towered like a crown. She bounced on her heels with the energy of someone who hadn't hit 20 yet.

"Kai," I received her with a measured smile. "Aren't you usually in classes on Wednesday mornings?"

"Teacher workday." She beamed, scooping up a notebook riddled with stickers. Kai followed me to my desk. "Plus, Ms. McKenzie said you might help with my project."

"What kind of project?" I set down my bag and gave her a questioning look.

"Oral history, remember? For a digital exhibit we're building with the Center—'Voices We Almost Lost.'" This child spoke with her hands as much as her mouth, continuing with, "I'm focusing on how silence moves through generations. You know, what gets lost and why."

Kai and I had met months ago, after I gave a brief talk for the Center's youth internship program. I'd been asked to speak about trauma response and memory preservation, but she was the only one who stayed behind to ask questions about language, displacement, and how stories mutate when families migrate. Since then, she'd made a habit of orbiting wherever I was seated.

"So," she said, already flipping through her chaotic notebook. "I want to record conversations with elders who've lived through major change—but I'm especially curious about what they leave *out*." She tapped a page. "You once said in that workshop that forgetting can be just as intentional as remembering. That blew my mind, Doc B. Like—what does it mean to survive if your story doesn't survive with you?"

I wasn't prepared for philosophy before coffee, but she hit a nerve with that one. The girl was sharper than I'd given her credit for. "You think I can help answer that?"

"I think you already have." She didn't even blink. "But I need to ask better questions this time."

"Then ask them," I smiled. "Maybe I'm finally ready to answer."

Kai's chewing paused for the first time, and she sat up straighter before leaning forward to share even more.

"So... my mom's a nurse. She says people remember things when their bodies are ready, not when they're asked. I still don't know what she's talking about, but...My grandfather stopped talking after he left Haiti. Never told my mom anything about his youth and the specifics of what made him flee. That sucks, you know? It left us with identity gaps, and now it's too late." She shrugged. Her gaze dropped for the first time. "That's why I care about stories that people don't know how to say out loud. Someone else likely needs to hear it."

She had no idea how close she was to the honest message I'd allowed myself to record that morning. I nodded. "You might be better at this than you think." At seventeen, Kai was precocious, earnest, and relentlessly curious. The kind of young person who exhausts adults with questions but makes them feel seen in a way few people manage.

She glanced up.

"Look, I really did just stop in to look for an old tape player," I told her. "But I'm not going to pretend I haven't been more active in giving light to more parts of my life lately."

Kai didn't speak. Just waited.

"I wrote written about other people for my entire career. I framed them. Protected them. But it is harder to tell your own story," I confessed while gathering my things.

"So... lunch?" The kid was hopeful.

"You know I'm retired, right?" I teased.

She tilted her head, studying me with unexpected perception. "I don't believe youuu, Doc B!" She almost sang her statement instead of saying it. "I don't think you want to stop contributing and working on this stuff completely. That's why you come here!"

"Ishhh, Kai!" I muttered, my mother tongue slipping out. I glanced at my watch. "I need to get going."

"Oh, come on! *Please.*"

This time I didn't hesitate. "Yes." I gave her a smile.

"Yes!" Kai looked like she was going to blow a bubble with her gum, but thank God, she didn't. "I won't keep you, Doc B, but I'll reach out to set it up. Thank you!

A cowardly voice whined that I should've said no. I had so many other things to do, a mystery tape calling me at home, and a thousand ways to justify keeping to myself. But Kai's earnestness tugged harder than my fear of being needed.

"Wait, can I ask one more thing?" Kai pleaded. "What made you come to Miami? Your bio says you were in DC at Georgetown for years, then suddenly moved here."

It was the kind of question that young people ask when they assume life moves in clean lines. Kai didn't mean any harm. That was the trouble with her—she never meant harm.

"Life changes," I said carefully. "Sometimes new beginnings require new geography."

Kai paused and looked at her sneakers. "I guess so. My mom says the same thing. She brought me here from Haiti. I miss my friends, but...it is safer here."

That was the first time she'd mentioned it. For all her openness, Kai rarely spoke about her own history. "That's a difficult trade-off but I've found that some distances give us perspective."

"Did you ever stop missing home?"

Which one? I wanted to respond but didn't. I just looked at her, this bright young girl with her boombox earring and multicolored notebook. "Sometimes. But eventually you build something new that's worth labeling home too."

She seemed disappointed but nodded. "Thanks for talking with me, Doc B. I'm looking forward to linking up with you when you have more time."

"Sounds good." I offered her a smile. "Until then, keep asking good questions."

Kai left with a wave, her smile now looking a little more satisfied. *Before I reached my apartment again, I pulled out my phone without even thinking about it. I swiped to the photo I'd taken of Ezra's personal card and initiated a call.*

"Dr. Bekele," he answered, amused. "You miss me already?"

Instant smile. I tucked a loose curl behind my ear and took the short flight of steps instead of the elevator so I didn't have to drop the call. *"Do you still have that cassette player you mentioned?"*

He chuckled, and I could picture the tilt of his mouth. "I do."

"Good." I let the pause stretch just long enough. "I might need it. And maybe a little help pressing play."

I ended the call and caught my reflection in the microwave door—eyes alert, mouth still curved. I ran a fingertip along my bottom lip, then shook it off like static and moved on. My fingers tingled from holding my cell too tight. And a bit of thirst crept in. I reached into the kitchen cabinet for an old cup from the Washington DC chapter of my life. The one I always saved for when I needed to remember that I was powerful enough to not only choose my own name and meaning but bring new life into this world. But my hand jerked hard in a sudden snap.

The cup slipped, hitting the counter first, then the floor. I heard it shatter before I saw it.

My breath caught in my chest. Shock. Disappointment. A little anxiety. I crouched down too quickly to clean up the mess and felt my balance falter as I reached for the biggest shard.

"Ouch!" A sharp edge caught the pad of my finger. Blood bloomed fast. Shit...shit, shit, shit!

I sucked in a breath and sat back on my heels. The sight of it all made me lightheaded. Embarrassed, too, though no one else was here.

"Is this how it's going to be now?" I mumbled. "Every time I try to move forward, something pulled me back." *Hasn't that been all of life?* My inner voice goaded me. Then I looked around the kitchen as if I didn't recognize it. Like the walls had shifted while I wasn't watching.

This was supposed to be a good day. A day I did something brave—I'd spoken a decades-old truth. I'd opened up to Kai, and I had called Ezra. So much progress... I'd opened a door. Yet, just like that... my body had reminded me it could slam shut just as fast.

I cleaned the cut with peroxide before wrapping it in gauze. Then I swept the broken pieces into a kitchen towel and tossed the whole thing into the trash. I didn't need the object to keep the memory. It was in my soul. When I sat back down, my apartment was louder. The hum of the fridge. The creak in the floorboard near the front door. Everything pushed in at the edges.

I straightened my spine and pulled out the cassette. Set it on the table in front of me. Ezra would be here soon.

I would not meet him shaken or weak.

5

WHAT IF I SPEAK

He arrived on time just like before, and I'd removed the bandage from my hand by the time he entered. I didn't want to draw more attention to my unruly body than necessary.

"Afternoon, Mae," Ezra beamed. He spotted a tilt in my rug instantly, nudging it straight with his foot before setting down the tape player. I gathered that was how he moved through the world – always noticing things that needed adjusting.

"Hi there," I smiled and gestured for him to have a seat.

He nodded pleasantly. "You sure you want to hear it?"

"I am."

"Been meaning to throw this old thing out, but now I'm glad I didn't." He dramatically pressed the buttons to ensure they worked. "Welp." He loaded the tape. "Shall we?" Ezra paused. "Wait a minute—want some privacy?"

I debated. I did, but I didn't want to ask him to wait outside. I wasn't sure what to say.

"I'll just, uh…hang back here if you don't mind. Or on your terrace." He read my mind.

I gave him a grateful smile and opened the patio door for him before returning to the table. My hands rattled when I finally pressed play. Static came first. Then my voice. I turned it up.

"This is Makeda Bekele, practicing formal speech patterns for an application review. Georgetown Fellowship, 1980."

I hadn't expected the cheerfulness, or the formality. I sounded like I was auditioning for someone else's life. The sound of it brought a wistful smirk to my face.

I glanced at Ezra. His back was to me as he looked out at the bay, but I felt he could still hear the recording…and was listening. The voice on the tape read from a dry script. Then, there was a tumble before silence, as if it had fallen or been put down. I heard papers shuffling.

"Why am I still recording?' My younger self sighed. "I don't think I'll submit this one. My accent won't sit right for them. It always softens when I talk about home."

I remembered the room. It was a borrowed apartment with thin blue walls, one suitcase, and minimal furniture. It was my first stop in DC after escaping the devastation happening to students in Ethiopia. More of my voice came from the tape…

"I keep thinking about Selam. She had a faster mind and sharper tongue than me. The kind of woman who could scare a man twice her size. We had planned to leave together.

And we thought we could. But at the last checkpoint, every-thing changed. A set of papers raised questions. The guard stared at them, then at us. He said only one of us would be allowed through and looked at me. I didn't move. And Selam, she...she didn't beg." There was a beat in the recording. "I told myself I'd go back," I heard myself say. "That I'd find her. I never did."

I gulped. Ezra's head hung down as if he were stretching his neck. By now, I wanted to call him in, so I didn't have to finish listening alone. I opened the door all the way and called quietly, "Ezra?"

He turned.

"You can come back now."

He didn't ask if I was sure. He just nodded once and stepped inside. Ezra closed the door behind him and stood nearby rather than sit. He could hear it clearly now.

I pressed play again... "I became someone else here... They call me Mae in this country. But back home...I was Makeda, and I was fire. I sang offkey and happy in court-yards. Drank wine in the morning. I kissed diplomats while carrying pamphlets in the same purse. I wanted to change everything. I still do. I just don't know *how* anymore. I don't even know who to *be* in this strange land." I'd paused. "What if I continue being the woman who speaks, even if my voice shakes. Even if no one listens. Especially then. What if?"

Click.

Ezra tapped the machine. He didn't speak right away, and I appreciated that more than he could know. Eventually, he asked, "That was you?"

"A long, long time ago, yes."

"Do you think you locked it away because it was honest?"

"I don't know. I have no idea."

"Did you ever tell anyone about her?" he queried but immediately looked like he regretted it.

"No. Who?" I didn't know if he was talking about young me, or Selam—the woman left behind.

"*You*."

"Oh. Yes. I was married once. Had a family. I wasn't always the way I am."

"Don't say it like that," he said effortlessly. You're fascinating." Ezra spoke so easily. So assuredly.

I had no words but a smile was fighting to play at my lips. I kept my eyes on the tape. This was a lot. "I let myself forget the sound of that version of me. The feel and energy of her. I don't like that."

Ezra sat back in his chair and shifted the conversation a bit. "You can digitize this. Clean up the audio and save it so you never lose it again."

I should, I thought. "Listen, Ezra. Thank you for this. I know this part isn't your job."

"Neither was giving you my personal number, Mae. I wanted to see you again. I still do."

What was I going to do with this man? He had no idea how much came with seeing me again. Honestly, I didn't remember saying any of the things on that tape. Funny how the decades cherry-pick memories. But the voice on the recording didn't lie. It carried too much breath and a swell of hope.

"Just coffee. Or tea," Ezra broke through my thoughts.

"Or anything you'd like to do that doesn't feel like pressure. What do you say, Mae? Will you go out with me?"

My mouth opened, then closed. My shoulders pulled inward. The voice on the tape *was* still in the room. So were the years I'd folded away.

Ezra waited without fidgeting. Just watching me like he could see all the moving pieces and wasn't afraid of where they might land.

"I'm not...easy..."

He tilted his head, a smile ghosting his mouth. "That's not what I asked."

"You don't know what you're asking."

"I'm asking for a little time with a fascinating woman who just made my chest hurt and my spine straighten. Coffee. That's all."

I looked down before I could smile.

Ezra rubbed his hands together and twitched his lips. "I've got a brother," he said. "Younger. Brilliant. More selfless. He handled the hard stuff in our family when I couldn't—or wouldn't. We haven't spoken in years."

I listened.

"I'm not always the version of myself I meant to be either," he added. "So...slow works for me."

I reached for the empty teacup on the table just to have something to do with my hands.

"I'll let you know," I said, but the words already felt like a lie. I knew I wanted to see him again too, but I was a bit afraid of doing too much too fast with everything else I had going on.

Ezra stood with a hopeful grin and slipped his bag over his shoulder. "Take care, Mae," he told me on his way out.

I nodded. "You, too."

Later that night, I couldn't stop myself if I tried. I texted him: *I can't tolerate Starbucks and whatever else Americans call coffee. How about Fairchild Gardens at twilight? Something different.*

Ezra replied immediately: *You couldn't have chosen a better place! Just tell me when.*

I will, I responded.

Big grin. I didn't stifle it this time. I lit one of my good candles. One of the ones I'd been saving because of a ridiculous belief I'd let attach itself to me over the years—that pleasure should wait—no more of that, I decided in that moment. The little torch filled the room with fig and something like honey. In that moment, I felt a small thrill at my own audacity. The stillness wasn't empty tonight. It shimmered like a slice of heaven. My hands were calm but aware. My mind was awash with vivid memories. And my heart stretched its legs.

I finally got up when I heard my noisy neighbors through the wall. They were too old to argue so much! To busy myself, I wiped down the table where Ezra and I had sat and put the tape away. I double-checked the kitchen for cleanliness, and I locked the patio door.

Then I did something I hadn't done in years. I reached for the long, rust-red wrap I used to wear when I danced. The one with a slit that caught wind when I turned. I hung it on the bedroom door. Just in case.

6

SAY YES TO JOY

Hearing my voice on that tape unearthed something in me down to the marrow in my bones. That woman was aching to resurface now. Being so bluntly reminded of the voice that once sang protest songs until a raw throat. Who'd pushed back on colonels and customs officers, on PTA moms who later called her "exotic," while asking to touch her hair. The one whose American bosses initially found her "hard to understand" was unextinguished despite my hands trembling over a tape player like nervous birds.

I reached for my voice recorder and began to capture how I felt while it was all still fresh.

"I don't feel like myself," I began. "Well, I do, but in an odd way. My body is buzzing in the wrong places. I need air but don't want to leave the house. I want company but freeze when I get the invite. I need silence to unpack last night, but I'm just pacing." I stopped. Exhaled.

"Key West," I mumbled, opening the fridge just to close it again. "God, I want to go. But I don't want to carry all this."

I poured a glass of wine and let my phone keep recording.

Each memo untied something knotted in me. It didn't necessarily feel good, but it felt like *truth*. I sat at the table, drink in hand, and tapped my screen just to see the light. No new messages. There goes the silence I said I wanted. It was louder than I could stand.

I stared at the phone and whispered, "Don't wait too long, Mae."

Time was ticking, and I needed to say yes to joy now. To move my body now. To finish anything unfinished or abandon it and move on now. By noon, I'd gotten dressed, stretched, and made a half-decent brew with breakfast. That's when Seble called. There was no greeting—just:

"We're painting tonight."

"I beg your pardon."

"Paint and sip. Eight o'clock. I'll send the address. Yemi and Almaz are excited! And you...you need something fun that doesn't require a thesis," she teased.

"Yes, yes, yes. I know you're right!"

"Of course I am. So, we want to hang out and do something this evening, Makeda." I could hear her smile through the line. "Wear something that won't get you kicked out of Wynwood."

I laughed. "Fine. But I'm not painting anything meaningful."

"Good. Keep your symbolism at home. See you at eight!"

She hung up before I could tell her about Ezra. About

our date. About something feeling new—not wild or reckless, just... a re-opening. I'd thought about it enough and was ready to share, but it would have to wait until I saw them.

I spent most of the day trying to stay out of my head. I called the pharmacy to refill my meds, then confirmed with my doctor that I wanted to start all the therapies he'd mentioned. I tried on two outfits and even opened the suitcase I'd meant to use for Key West just to make it all more real.

By five, I caught myself playing an old record while humming along to a song from the 80s. And when I got to the paint and sip studio, I was greeted with bright lights and an echo of women choosing between wine, brushes, and canvas sizes. Someone had pre-ordered a cheese board. Someone else had brought extra aprons "just in case."

"Makeda Bekele! Did you stretch first?" Yemi was already seated when I arrived, swirling red wine with unnecessary ceremony.

Lord, here we go.

Almaz leaned over her easel, whispering, "Don't mind her, she's just bitter because she was banned from using glitter at the last event."

"I said it was biodegradable!" Yemi hissed, then turned to me with mock serenity. "You look good. Like a woman who might stir up some trouble!"

"How you figure?" I pulled the stool closer to the canvas. "And why are we painting fruit that looks like... this?"

Seble pointed to the instructor's "still life" model—three eggplants, two bananas, and one very suggestive cucumber standing upright.

"He, he, he, heeeeee!" The three of them cackled in unison.

"Let's just say we chose the risqué class and not the nude model. Though frankly, that might've been less subtle."

Almaz raised her wine. "To fertility metaphors we did not ask for."

"To fertile imaginations," I chimed in, touching my glass to theirs.

We laughed too loud. We ignored the instructor. We painted eggplants that looked like question marks and bananas with existential crises. For the second time this week, I let myself be ridiculous without apology, and it felt so, so good!

Halfway through, Seble leaned in. "So. You are glowing."

"Glowing?" I blushed.

"She means someone met someone," Yemi wagged her brush.

"The locksmith?" Almaz pressed.

"Who told you that?"

"You did!"

I paused, dipped back into the violet paint. "I might have a date."

Three gasps. One clink of glass.

"When?"

"Where?"

"Why now?"

I let the questions land and waited until they settled.

"His name is Ezra," I said finally. "Tomorrow. We're going to the botanical garden."

Seble's smile widened. "About time! Makeda, you are too

beautiful to have a half-empty bed," she scolded while wreaking havoc on the peel of her banana painting.

"You said you weren't going to paint anything meaningful," Almaz added, nudging me.

I looked down at my canvas. My eggplant looked drunk and emotionally unavailable.

"Just my type," I jested.

The evening danced on with so much laughter, warmth, and honesty that I was beside myself when it ended. My friends were exactly what I'd needed that night and only the pull of fatigue made me finally decide to call it an evening. With hugs and kisses, we parted with promises to ensure everything was ready for the Key West trip. It was inching closer, and we wanted it to go off without a hitch. I was all in.

THE NIGHT AIR hugged me differently after the merriment. I reached my car and fumbled for my keys. The lot was dim but not empty—some stragglers lingered, chatting near a food truck parked at the corner. Music drifted from it, soft and bassy. I smiled to myself once again. I only laughed that way when I was with my girls. I wasn't ready for it to end.

When I opened the driver's side door and angled in to sit, my right leg hesitated. It froze, then twitched. *Oh no.* A fast, sharp tremor rippled from knee to ankle. It was unmistakable. *No, no, no.* I steadied myself against the doorframe and waited. My friends had already gone because I said I was fine. I waited. Waited more. *Come on, please don't do this.* I begged my body.

It passed in seconds, thank Allah, but my heart raced longer. I sat down slowly, letting the door close harder than intended. The car was quiet except for my breath, and I placed both hands on the steering wheel while staring ahead. I braced for another wave, but it didn't come.

Still, I stayed parked for a while.

A different group of women crossed in front of my headlights laughing with an easy rhythm. Maybe in their 30s and 40s. So young and agile. I envied them. Not bitterly. Just with the kind of ache that hides behind the ribs. Damn it.

7

ALMOST ORDINARY

I loved the *sound* of early mornings. I'd been up since five, stretching, lifting light weights, and playing Nina Simone low enough to not wake the neighbors. Everything today felt *right*. It had been nearly a week since I felt the sting of envy stir from seeing those young women, but I was already glistening by sunrise. Envy is best repurposed as action. I didn't need an audience to affirm my belief—just movement, breath, and consistency.

By 7:00 a.m., I'd poured my coffee, worked out and showered, and walked barefoot across the cool tile toward what I now call my listening room. It used to be a guest room, then a storage chamber, then something in between. Until recently... I had the walls painted something close to deep ochre to deepen the quiet in here.

Moments after settling in, I remembered Kai had sent a message last night. Something about an event at the Cultural Center this weekend. She wanted to record interviews with "elders who hold history" as part of a passion project that might turn into a bigger film later. Lord, help me! I tapped out a quick reply: "Sure. What time, and what kind of questions are you asking?" I added a coffee cup emoji. She'd tease me for that.

Just as I hit send, my phone buzzed. It was a notification from the Coral Gables arts calendar. I'd forgotten I'd subscribed. There was a photo featured on the homepage—some soft-focus event at a gallery opening. And there, nearly blurred out in the corner of the frame was the image of a man who was unmistakable. My heart thudded and my eyes misted. It was only his profile—the line of his jaw—but I'd know that posture anywhere. It was my son, and he was holding hands with a woman whose back was to the camera. A slender beauty with an elegant updo. I stared at the photo, not breathing.

Alex. Confirmed by the tiny text in the photo's italicized caption. *Alex Jeffrey Jones and Nyla Baines, the power couple behind The Jeffrey Hotel.*

I stared at the picture for more than a minute, studying her posture, her hand on his. So polished. So public. She was lovely, I could admit that. A perfect match for the persona he'd curated. Flawless and feline on his arm.

I didn't click the article. The headline told me enough. What mattered wasn't in the story but in the frosted distance he'd kept. The way my son could be this close without a word made my heart ache. He was here. In my city. Still choosing not to see me. I sighed, letting the emotions course through me rather than trying to kick them out just for them to resurface at the wrong time later. I let my body feel and process what it must in real time because you cannot outrun your darkness or the dungeons of your soul. It was a skill I'd learned over the years.

I closed the tab, locked my phone, and walked toward the kitchen. Feeling. I rubbed my forehead as I took stock of my sustenance options. There was stew in the fridge and leftover wine from Seble's last visit. But I didn't want to eat alone today. I needed company to stitch myself back into the world, so I pulled out my phone again and scrolled to Ezra's last message. *Fairchild Gardens still sounds nice if you're free tonight. Twilight or just before?*

He replied in seconds: *I'm free, and just before to have better light. I can pick you up. Dress however you feel best.*

I smiled and shook my head. What did that even mean? Still, I replied: *I will meet you there. Wear your good boots. I will judge you if they're dusty.*

He wrote back: *Then I'll make sure they're perfect. Or just dusty enough!*

I closed my phone and finally exhaled. Yes! I had something else to look forward to. Something fun. Something exciting. Something *mine*.

Later that morning, Kai responded like she'd just popped out of bed. "Doc, B!" Such an exuberant child. "It's a community storytelling thing. Everyone's doing glossy reels—mine's gonna be black and white, real moody. Can you come Saturday? I would be so honored to highlight you. Also, 🐱 @ the coffee emoji. Didn't know you knew how to use those!"

Boy, did I remember being that age! I fired back a reply: *Send me the details. I'll be there.* I was energized to grip the reins of my life while mentoring another who wanted me in theirs. Kai reminded me what curiosity looked like before consequence wore it down. She was a bright young soul, and I admired that. And now, I could focus on my date with Ezra.

THE GARDEN WAS ALREADY HALF-COVERED in shadow by the time I arrived. I hadn't been to this place in a while, but was always enamored when I returned. A part of Miami for close to a century, Fairchild Gardens was filled with giant trees, secretive grottos, entwined sculptures, and yearning plants. I loved the spectacle of it all. The air smelled like ginger and wet bark, and a saxophonist near the north entrance was warming up for the evening concert. I adjusted my silk kimono, stepped around a broken mosaic tile, and spotted Ezra before he spotted me.

He wore a clean gray shirt and what I could only assume were the "good" boots. "You clean up alright," I teased him.

He turned and grinned. "I wasn't trying to impress you. Just the trees."

Cheeky. And cute. We walked slowly, with gravel giving under our feet. A kid ran past us chasing a balloon shaped like a butterfly while her father followed, out of breath. He laughed and apologized as he whizzed by.

"You've got that look again," Ezra said after a beat.

"What look?"

"The one that says you're reading everything and keeping score."

"I do not keep score!"

"That's a lie," he said without missing a beat. "Your eyes tally even when your mouth doesn't move."

Ha! I let a silence sit between us for a moment. The saxophonist hit a blue note that lingered, daring us to slow down.

I restarted our dialogue. "Ezra, first off, thank you for asking me out. I should have said that already. It's been a long time since I've done anything like this," I confessed. "Second, do you ever wish you'd picked a different line of work?" My question surprised even me. I didn't bother to keep the score dialogue going.

He shrugged. "I don't normally ask clients out," he said earnestly. "I'm just glad I took the chance and that you said yes...eventually. If nothing else, this moment was worth it. And to answer your question, yes. I used to, but not anymore. I fix what people lock up. In a weird way, that gives me a kind of clarity."

I raised an eyebrow. "That sounds rehearsed."

He stopped walking. "You want honesty or style?"

"Both," I replied. "But in the right order. And something to drink. Do you mind if we stop?"

He looked embarrassed that I had to say it first, but it really wasn't a problem for me. I was thirsty. "My apologies, Mae." He gestured. "Of course, let's get something!" Ezra wiped his brow and led the way.

A breeze lifted the edge of my kimono. Ezra looked at me differently then—less amused, more searching.

"Something about that family with the balloon caught you," he said as we ambled to a café tucked between palm trees. "I saw it in your face." Ezra pulled out a chair for me and waited until I was seated before sitting himself—an old-fashioned courtesy I hadn't experienced in years.

"I was a mother once," I said after we'd ordered. The words tumbled out before I could stop them. Way too raw. Damn it. "I still am, technically. But not in practice," I told him. I had to, given that I'd just requested honesty myself. Although I completely lacked style. I was rusty at dating.

Ezra's eyes held mine. "A son...or daughter?"

"A son." I nodded. I didn't want to continue, thinking I'd be a huge red flag, but I was in it now. "We're not really in touch though." The truth tasted bitter.

"Mmph."

How could I salvage this?

Before he could respond further, a small commotion erupted near the garden's central fountain. A cluster of people had gathered, their voices rising in delighted exclamations.

"What's happening?" I asked with a shock of delight. The interruption was perfect.

"The night-blooming cereus must be opening. They're quite rare."

"Night-blooming cereus?" I had no clue what he was talking about.

"The garden staff announced it just before you arrived. 'Queen of the night!'" he continued. "They bloom for just a few hours once a year, usually after sunset. It's supposed to be spectacular. Come, Mae!" Childlike enthusiasm popped through his previously measured demeanor.

"Okay, let's go." I found myself smiling at his unexpected eagerness.

Ezra quickly settled our bill with cash, and we joined the flow of visitors making their way to a glass structure. Small lights illuminated a gangly, unremarkable cactus plant draped over a support. But at its tips, several large white blooms slowly unfurled. Their petals gradually spread to reveal intricate centers.

"They look like they're breathing," I murmured, genuinely awed by the sight.

"They are, in a way," Ezra stood close enough that I could feel his warmth without touching. "The whole process takes about two hours. The scent will grow stronger as they open fully. It's really feminine, in a way. Masculine, too, in the back. All of life is in these flowers. I like plants. Got a little garden at home, myself!" Ezra was beside himself, just rambling.

Around us, strangers shared whispered observations, took photographs, pointed out details. There was something intimate about standing in this crowd, watching something so ephemeral with someone I barely knew.

"I've lived in Miami for twenty years, and I've never seen this."

"It's easy to miss the beauty in temporary things," Ezra replied, still watching the flower. "Most of us are too busy looking for what lasts."

I glanced at him. "Hmm. A poetic locksmith with a penchant for flowers, got it." *And what's wrong with looking for what lasts? I wondered.*

His smile reached his eyes now. "Locks are just puzzles with history. Poetry isn't so different. And flowers, well, you've got to be a weirdo to not appreciate them!"

A garden docent began sharing facts about the plant – its native habitats, its blooming patterns, the folklore surrounding it. Ezra and I stood listening, occasionally exchanging glances when something particularly interesting was mentioned. The heaviness of our earlier conversation dissipated in this shared moment of wonder. By the time we wandered back through the greenery, darkness had truly fallen. Ezra's statement still rang in my ear. I wanted to sit with that later to see what it meant for me rather than asking him for a deeper explanation. Our conversation flowed more easily now — about plants and about Miami's hidden treasures. About the music that still floated through the night air.

"I should probably be heading home," I yawned, though with genuine reluctance.

"May I walk you to your car?"

"Please do." I wanted to touch his hand but didn't.

We strolled unhurriedly, and I found myself appreciating his silent companionship as much as our conversation. Here was a man who somehow managed to be a chatterbox but didn't feel pressed to fill *every* moment with words.

At my car, he paused. "Thank you for this evening, Mae. I'd like to do it again sometime."

"I'd like that too."

"Perhaps somewhere with fewer natural urgencies," he suggested with a hint of humor.

"I don't know," I countered, surprising myself with a small laugh. "It made for a memorable first date."

His smile deepened at my acknowledgment of what this had been. "That it did." He took a hesitant half-step forward as if to reach for a hug but held back. Unsure.

"Thanks, again, Ezra." I took his hand softly in mine. I wish I could have the effect I used have to on men, but I was so much more awkward these days. It had been too long.

"The pleasure was all mine." He brought my hand to his lips and planted a sweet kiss.

Very old school. I liked it.

As I drove home with the streetlights flickering past, my hands were easy on the wheel. I pulled into my parking space, the engine ticking softly as it cooled. Then my phone buzzed once. One name: Alex Jones.

I stared at the screen.

It wasn't a message. It wasn't a missed call. It was real-time. *What on Earth did he want?*

8

GHOST LINES

I let his name bloom and wither on the screen as my phone rang for two loops. Alex...Alex...the name made me breathe like I was doing something wrong. My heartbeat stalled, then lurched. I thought about it... thought about answering, but I couldn't do it. Not so spontaneously. Instead, I pressed decline.

Something flinched under my rib as minutes peeled by like wallpaper. I sat in my parking space staring at the tiny envelope icon in my notification bar. "Alex..." I heard myself whisper.

His name lit every maternal nerve, but I choked the reflex. The car felt hot and the silence after his call rang out. My eyes squeezed shut and I pressed the phone to my chest in a half-cry, half-tremble. It felt like a bandage that couldn't hold against an old scar splitting open again.

I opened my eyes again. My son? It had been *years*. He knew where I lived. He never reached out, yet he had my number. Alex chose absence like it made him holy. Why was he calling now? I shuddered and opened my car door, pushing through the stiffness and ache that suddenly surged in my body.

Why.

Now?

I moved more intentionally, trying to relive my beautiful hours with Ezra instead of the few seconds from Alex that punctured it. But the call made me unsteady. I set my bag down and fought to return to the garden instead of reality, but it was a struggle. I was no match for the body blow of absence resurging. The damn call had ruptured something deep.

I checked the time. *8:37.* I had a trip planning meeting with my friends in the morning. A doctor's appointment after that. Kai was expecting me over the weekend, too. I needed my rest to deal with them all. Still, I was suddenly overwhelmed by questions of what he could have possibly wanted. My body tensed as I unsuccessfully tried to wind down. Before I could fully shower and climb into bed, the cell phone lit up on my nightstand with another call.

Robert Jones.

That name felt like a bullhorn. And now I was really worried, because *he* only showed up when something shifted —maybe in him, maybe in me.

I answered. "Robert?"

"Mae," he responded, like he'd been waiting all year to say it. His voice hadn't changed. Still smooth, unhurried. "I hope this isn't a bad time."

"It's a rather peculiar time, honestly." I wondered if our son had called him too.

A pause. I could almost hear him debating whether to lead with small talk or something real. And I was dying for the latter.

"You've been on my mind," he said finally. "How are you?"

"Um... " I adjusted my position to be more upright. "I—I'm fine, Robert. What... I mean... how about you? What's going on?" I tripped over my words, not even remotely ready to tell him the truth about my life. We had divorced amicably, and I hadn't seen him in decades, but he still called me a few times a year to check in.

"I'm okay. Still working with the housing co-op, though I'm pretending I might retire this year," he told me. I could hear the smile in his voice. "Busy. And a little tired. That kind of tired that's just part of the body now."

Small talk. Alright. That's what we're going with.

I laughed quietly, waiting for the real reason for his call. "That sounds familiar."

"I figured it might."

Another pause.

"Are you sure you're alright? I just have this feeling, and I wanted to hear your voice."

"I'm fine. Keeping busy. You know how it is."

"Not really," he said. "I was never as good at doing five things at once."

I smiled. "You were better at finishing the ones that mattered."

"Aweeee." There was a silence. "Okay. Well...have you heard from Alex lately?"

The question was an electric jolt. *Was something wrong? Why had both of them called me tonight?* I had so many questions, and I wouldn't tell a lie.

"He called. Today."

Robert inhaled sharply. "He *what*?"

"Alex dialed my number. Not long ago, as a matter of fact."

"After all this time?"

"Yes."

"Did you answer?"

"I couldn't."

"Why?"

"Because I've forgotten how to speak to someone who's already made peace with not wanting me. With me being dead to them."

"Mae..."

"I'm not angry," I told him. "But I do wonder what he wants from me now. What made him curl his fingers around a phone and call me on this night."

"I don't know. I wish I could say, but I don't."

"Did he call you?"

"No. Not at all." His answer was fast and honest. "Not since my birthday."

The words scorched, but it wasn't Robert's fault. "Well, at least you got that." Tears welled in my eyes.

"I'm sorry, Mae. I don't know where I went wrong with him."

"You didn't. He is his own person, with his own dreams

for what his life should be and..." I trailed off. I had no other excuses or rationalizations to offer.

Robert didn't try to fill the silence. I rolled my wrists and ankles to free myself from more stiffness building up.

"It's cruel, Mae. What he's done. You don't have to explain it away."

The words unleashed the tears I'd been holding for years. They breached the dam. "If I don't try to make sense of it, I'll come undone," I confessed. "And I can't afford that kind of unraveling right now." This was all so much, so soon. "I have other things to worry about."

"Then don't unravel," Robert spoke gently. "But don't protect him either. You don't owe him that anymore."

I would never.

"Although, I'm sure you won't," Robert added, as if he just remembered who he was talking to. "And...what's worrying you?"

I wiped under my eyes with the back of my hand. The heat behind them was real. "Nothing I can't handle, but thank you for saying that."

"I should've said it sooner."

A softness returned to his voice. Its gentleness gave me permission to backtrack and actually tell him more about what I had going on. I told him about my diagnosis, and that I was taking it seriously. That I was reclaiming old parts of me and defining new ones. And... that I'd started something —likely a book—and it was coming out in fragments, voice notes, half-pages. All I knew was that I needed to tell my story before my body wouldn't let me.

Robert went quiet for too long, then simply said, "I'm

glad you shared that." His voice held no pity, just presence, and that made me feel steadier even if strangely exposed. "Regardless of anything, Mae. I'm always here for you."

And then there was a somber quiet on the line.

"Still dancing?" I tried to ease us both out of the ache and confusion.

"Ha!" Robert was grateful for the diversion. "Every Friday. Church basement. Bad speakers, good knees."

That warmed me in a beautiful way. I did still love this man. Just platonically now. "Good for you."

Robert and I used to have such an amazing time. Decades ago or not, I would never forget his moves on dance floors. Broad shoulders, quick feet, and those ridiculous blond curls that always flopped into his blue eyes mid-spin—no rhythm, but charm for days. There was still a part of me that couldn't believe I'd come to America and fallen in love with a white man, but I did. And initially, I'd fallen hard because he was just so beautiful and perfect. He made me feel safe when every day felt like a duel between the old me and the one I was trying to figure out how to become. We'd actually met at a house party back in DC. Robert had traded events and nightclubs with sticky floors for sanctified holy rooms now, but that was fine. It worked for him.

"It's good to hear your voice, Mae. It really is. Although, I'm sorry I caught you on the heels of the hurricane that is our son. And I'm very sorry about your diagnosis."

"Not your fault. If anything, your voice helps."

"I appreciate that."

Before I could say another word, my phone vibrated with a text message from Ezra.

"Well...I won't keep you, Mae. Just promise me you'll take care of yourself. And call me if anything changes with Alex. I'll call him, too. I won't bring you up unless you want me to."

"Don't." My words were a razor.

"Figured you'd say that."

"Of course."

He lingered half a second longer, then the line disconnected.

Robert... I sighed to myself. He and I didn't have a bad marriage. That was the problem. It was a peaceful but misaligned life. Gentle on the surface, but never quite rooted in the same soil, so we lovingly let each other move on.

I then looked down to finally see Ezra's message: *Such a good time with you. I can't wait to do it again. Goodnight.*

My heart warmed and my shoulders relaxed. The words were everything in that moment to stabilize the whiplash of the last hour. *Goodnight,* I typed back.

9

UNRETURNED CALLS

Sleep was fitful and mostly elusive. I was uncomfortable in my skin, and my hands shook like children afraid of the dark. Sweat drenched me. I hadn't dealt with night perspiration in years. My body was hot but my thoughts were cold. Somewhere beneath the pain and disappointment, I still wanted Alex to call again. In one of my dreams, I saw four-year-old him crawling into one of my lecture halls after class. He'd gotten loose from Robert and followed my voice. The visuals rattled me.

I didn't know what scared me more—him wanting something, or him wanting nothing at all. Years of silence, and now a missed call. Without an explanation. Without any context. Just a vague voicemail from a child who made me feel like a failure as a mother. What I heard when I played the message was a son who hesitated when he said, "Hi... um...mom. It's Alex. I thought it might be time we talked. If that's something you'd be open to."

"What the hell was I supposed to do with that?" I fussed as I began dressing for the day. *If that's something you'd be open to.* Hmph! "What's next—'Press one to accept emotional responsibility?'" My emotions were a tangled mess.

The more I recalled of his short message, the more uneasy I felt. But I had to try not to get too worked up and trigger stress responses in my body. Maybe he was getting married. Maybe he was having a child. Hell, maybe he wanted closure, or absolution, or a final box ticked before standing in front of someone else's mother.

Or maybe it had nothing to do with me. Perhaps I was just... next on a list. In any case, I was not ready to call him back. I didn't even know what I would say. Instead, I sat at my desk and picked up a pen. With just a blank page and the weight of a moment I hadn't expected, I wrote:

What does a mother say to a child who ghosted her while still alive? Do you ask what they want, or what took them so long? Do you let them come back empty-handed, or do you ask for something you can feel?

I had no answers. I just let the questions sit there while I let my skin and blood feel every emotion they needed to before I finished dressing and headed out to my doctor and then to meet Kai. I had my own life to focus on.

Yemi had texted earlier, *"Planning brunch moved to Seble's place. 11 sharp. Just to wrap up the final details and ensure we all agree."*

I stared at the message. Then at the clock. Then back at the message. I typed and erased three different responses before settling on: *"Can't make it. Not feeling great this morning.*

Tell the girls I'll catch up later." It wasn't a lie. Just incomplete. I was overwhelmed.

Yemi was understanding and said she would relay the message.

Dr. Greene entered with a half-formed apology already on his lips. "Sorry, Mae. I had a procedure that ran long and a resident who forgot what 'urgent' means," he offered a smile but didn't sit. "How are you feeling today?"

What a loaded question, I thought, but grateful someone asked. "I feel functional. A little foggy. Still myself, just... harder to steer."

He paused before responding. "That sounds exhausting. Let's see what we can do to make it less so." He used his foot to nudge over a stool to take a seat before swiping through his tablet. "Have you been taking your meds?"

"Not as consistently as I should be. I'm not used to taking something every day. But I will be sure not to miss another day."

"Great. That's important, Mae. It'll help with your symptoms," he told me.

I nodded, and he continued with a few more questions before landing on, "Okay...I've reviewed your latest reports. The tremor's a little more frequent. Your handwriting sample looked tighter, but a motor delay was obvious in the final lines."

I crossed my arms. "And the voice thing?"

He looked up. "Your cadence has shifted a bit. I noticed it last time. You're pausing more before certain words."

I didn't blink. I could barely breathe. I could hear the old, white, circular clock ticking across the room.

"I want to keep monitoring for cognitive changes," Dr. Greene continued. "It's possible we're not looking at classic Parkinson's," he paused to look me in the eyes. "It could be one of the atypicals—Parkinson's Plus or another variant— but we won't jump to that yet. I'm scheduling additional imaging."

My heart sank. "So, what do I do in the meantime?"

"Therapy. Document symptoms. Don't wait to report new changes. And..." He hesitated. "Have someone who knows your baseline. Someone you trust to speak for you if things accelerate."

That one hit differently. "Okay." I nodded stiffly. *Tick. Tock.*

"Will do, thank you." I stood and straightened my scarf. My legs didn't feel weak this time, which somehow made me angrier. I didn't know what to do with that mix of clarity and dread. Outside, the Miami heat smacked into me, thick with humidity. I took one breath, then another, and kept walking. *This is life. This is. Just. Life.*

There was nothing left to process in the lobby. I didn't want to cry in my car, and I didn't want to go home. So, I kept driving. Toward the camera. Toward the girl who keeps asking the right questions, even when I'm not ready. Kai's film project now mattered more than it had an hour ago. I texted her: *"Running five minutes behind. Are you still good for the shoot?"*

She replied fast: *"Yup! I'm excited! Please don't bail, Doc."*

She had no idea how much I needed her not to say the right thing. Just something real. I drove over.

Kai had sent a list of potential interview questions. Half of them were far too ambitious, the other half too vague. But she was trying. She'd also hinted that she might want to shoot me in my home to diversify the footage and make it feel more personal. I liked the idea.

The a.m. air was damp and heavy, but the breeze was cool through my linen clothing. I'd put on lipstick to feel like my face still belonged to me, and tried to hum along with music as I moved through the mild traffic on the way to the Center. Still, I drove slower than I needed to, haunted. The vibration of Alex's call still thrummed in my bones. I reached the Cultural Center and crossed the plaza toward the side entrance. That's where Kai had said she'd meet me. She wasn't there yet.

A voice called out to someone behind me. "Hey—Reed!"

I turned, but the sound wasn't for me. A man was stepping out of a supply truck, hand raised to greet someone inside the building. He wore scuffed work boots and a faded long-sleeve shirt rolled up at the forearms. A toolbelt sagged slightly at his hip.

He noticed me looking.

"Sorry," he said, catching my eye with an easy nod. "Didn't mean to startle you."

He had Ezra's dimple. The same crooked smile, though slower to arrive.

I tilted my head slightly. "Reed?"

He shrugged, adjusted the toolbelt at his hip. "Yeah. Luther."

That was all he offered. Before I could respond, the side door creaked open and Kai came bouncing out with two clipboards and a giant camera bag. Her braids were adorned with gold accessories.

"There you are!" she chirped. Then saw Luther. "Oh—sorry, didn't mean to interrupt."

"Nah, you're good, young lady," he quipped. Luther stepped aside with a nod.

Kai handed me a document. "We're set up inside—Room B. Got an extra mic just in case. Are you ready?" She chewed her gum like a goat.

"Almost." My eyes were still on the man walking back toward a shiny supply truck.

He moved like someone who once walked faster. As he reached the open door, I heard him mutter into a phone—low, irritated, and not for us. "No. I don't talk to him like that anymore. Try Ezra yourself."

That name landed in my chest like a dropped plate.

He didn't look back.

He didn't know me.

But I'd gathered enough now. The last name. The build. The complexion. The way that single dimple flashed when he almost smiled. Luther was clearly Ezra's estranged brother, and now I had a question I didn't know how—or when—to ask.

I watched Luther's back disappear behind the truck's dusty open door. He wasn't curious about anything behind him and went on about his day. Meanwhile, the tail end of a call I wasn't supposed to hear rocked me.

Ezra's brother reminded me of how small the world is. And how silent everyone else could be, not just me. Their fracture was deep but felt more jagged at the edges coming from Luther's aura. What else should I know about Ezra? Why would someone like him, so—

"Okaaayy." Kai snatched me out of my thoughts. She dragged out the vowel like a grand-opening ribbon as we stepped inside. "What was *that* face about?"

"Which face?"

"The one you made when that old man said Ezra. Do you know him?"

Old man. I gave her a forced smile and pushed through the door. "Room B, wasn't it?"

Kai squinted. She knew I wasn't answering but didn't push. Her clunky earrings jingled as she shifted her bag and bounded ahead.

The room smelled like warm plastic and old paper inside. A box fan rattled in the corner while another spun lazily above. Folding chairs lined the walls like nervous spectators. And Kai dropped her gear like she owned the place.

"Alright," she exhaled, wiping her hands against her relaxed-fit jeans. "We're recording three people's stories today. Everyone has ten minutes. I really want you to go last, Doc B."

I raised a brow. "Why, Kai?"

"Because you're the climax!" She grinned. "And because the woman from Haiti gets super shy unless she knows more people will be in. You're the headliner," she spoke excitedly. "I brought snacks!" She popped open a bag of mini Kit Kats and tossed me one without warning. I caught it on reflex. "Did you think about doing that extra section at your place?" Her eyes begged for a yes.

"Yes. Let's do it."

A knock interrupted us. An older gentleman I'd never seen—slender, Caribbean accent, red cap, and loud car keys —peeked in.

"Are you de one doin' de oral history?"

Kai stepped forward. "Yes! Are you Dr. Mehu?"

"No. Mehu is running late. I am just the driver for de day. Helpin' out, you know? Name's Clive." He tilted his head. "You have any water in here?" he asked with a Jamaican accent.

"Yes. It's in the hallway, near the fire extinguisher," I told him, and then he slipped out.

Kai blinked. I said nothing. Just unwrapped the chocolate treat she'd given me.

"So..." she shifted her tone. "Yes! Thanks for agreeing to an extra shoot. We can sort it out later. And Doc B?"

"Yes?"

"I want to ask you something. It's for after the interviews, but you can start thinking about it now."

I waited.

"Have you ever thought of writing all of this down, like, *really* writing it? Not just notes and sidebars for classrooms or courtrooms—but a book. Your life. The revolutions. The silence. The parts they don't teach. So no one forgets."

I looked at her.

She was seventeen. Still full of bounce and nerve and

chaotic brilliance. But she saw something real, and said it plain.

I stood, brushing imaginary lint from my shirt. "Yes, actually, I have, Kai. Just recently, and I've started making some notes."

"OMG! Yes, yes!" She was pleased by my words.

"Get your mic ready, Kai," I chuckled. I had so many other things on my mind that I couldn't indulge the book idea more in the moment and wanted to ensure we got through what I'd come in for today. Meanwhile, thoughts of at least four men boomeranged in my mind. I needed time with my sister-friends after this.

"All set," she gestured to her cameras and sat down to begin.

I walked to the front of the room. The mic clicked on. A red light blinked. The fan stuttered off in the corner. Outside the window, the supply truck had long rumbled off but Luther was still floating into my thoughts. As we got going with the interview, my pulse skipped from the whirlwind of it all.

Kai's voice buzzed through my earpiece. "You're live."

I started slow, with my name, background, and a fragment of why I stayed in the field of forensic linguistics and archival history work even after retirement. I let my voice land with authority, but inside, I was shrinking and scanning at once. Kai's questions were simple. Until they weren't.

"How do you know when a memory is worth keeping?" she quizzed from the corner.

I blinked.

"It's not about worth," I said to the camera. "It's about

consequence. Some memories punish you for keeping them. Others punish you when you forget."

The room went still. *Was that too much for these kids?*

Kai didn't say anything for a few beats. Then: "What do you do with the ones that keep changing their shapes?"

"I name them anyway. And then I live with the echo." That was supposed to be the end of the segment. But my voice kept going. "I need to write more of this down specifically," I heard myself say. The words felt like thunder when they left my lips.

A chair shift in the corner. Kai hadn't expected that answer. Neither had I. The truth was, the more I spoke, the more comfortable I felt about documenting my life for myself and others in print and on film. I had no idea how to formally write a book that wasn't academic, but the idea of it felt more and more solidified with each day—as if I needed one more thing to manage. But I would. I didn't have time *not* to.

When the recording ended, Kai and I politely wrapped up before I headed out. We promised to reconnect for adding the new footage in a week or so. Then, my cell rang with a call from Yemi about going to a dance class this weekend and our upcoming trip.

"That sounds like fun," I smiled at the thought of music and motion again.

"I thought you'd like it. Best of all, the first class is free this Saturday morning."

"Yes, let's do it!"

"Mm hm. It will be a great precursor to our trip in two weeks."

"Key West. Yes. Absolutely," I told her, feeling better about it all. "Listen, Yemi, I want to make this trip about more than wine and a good time."

"Oh?"

"Yes." I hesitated. "I want to read something to you all. One of the essays I've been working on."

The line went quiet. She was surprised.

"...Wait, for real? You never read us anything before."

"Positive. If I don't say it out loud soon, I'm afraid I'll never say it at all."

"Alright. I'm excited to hear it then!"

I smiled. "Thank you. I have to run now. I'll catch up with you soon."

WHEN I ARRIVED at my apartment building, I saw Ezra waiting in reception. I'd completely forgotten he was coming by. He smiled when he saw me. It was easy and familiar. Too easy. He didn't yet know that I'd have questions for him. I didn't even know if I had the energy to ask them, honestly. The sight of Ezra's dimple reminded me about the man I'd met earlier in the day. Luther.

"Right on time," Ezra announced. "I won't be long unless you want me to be. Just came to grease that special box of yours so it doesn't seize up on you again. You look lovely, Mae!" he complimented as he followed me into the elevator.

Ezra looked dusty and tired, yet still handsome. The box was out, and the light coming through my blinds split across the floor in hard slats. He was a little quieter than usual and worked quickly as I set my things down. That part of him hadn't changed. But I had. The doctor's words clung to the back of my neck with claws. I stood behind him, staring at the outline of his ear and how it flowed down to his jawline. So perfect. *Sigh.* My throat felt too small but I squeezed the words out.

"You okay, Mae? You're rather quiet."

"I'm all right," I lied. I did not want to talk about what I'd just learned. It was too much too soon. In fact, I deflected. "Just a few things on my mind."

"Like what?" A beat.

He glanced over his shoulder. "Hm?"

"I um...I think I met your brother today."

Ezra stilled. One hand on the box, the other curled around a soft cloth. Ezra looked up, but not at me.

"What? Where?"

"At the Cultural Center."

He finally faced me, concerned.

"He didn't say much," I continued. "But I recognized the dimple. The way he stood. You favor each other very much."

Ezra nodded once. Jaw tight. I gave him space to fill in the silence, but he didn't.

"He said your name like it didn't belong to him anymore," I kept going. "Like something he gave up without a second thought."

Ezra rose slowly, hands at his sides. "Yeah, well, remember I told you that we haven't spoken in a long time."

"Why?"

He didn't answer at first. I wanted to push but remembered the grace he gave me. But I couldn't help myself. "What happened between you two?"

Ezra shifted his weight and looked at the box, then to the floor. "Not everything broken needs naming or fixing, Mae."

His pivot felt like a boomerang of Alex. Of *me*. Maybe it was the whiplash of emotions I'd felt throughout the day. Maybe it was my own demons circling and screeching too close to the surface. I wasn't sure, but I just couldn't stop myself from pushing. "I'm not asking for his version," I responded.

"I know."

"I want yours."

His eyes locked on mine.

"Then you're asking too much."

Ezra began packing up with no further words. He walked to the door, and I didn't stop him. I had enough to deal with. Let him go.

"I'll see you," he mumbled before leaving. When the door closed behind him, I remained there with arms still crossed, the box still sitting open and polished. The silence wasn't peaceful. It pressed in. It echoed all the things left unsaid in that office earlier. All the things I didn't want to face. And for the first time all day, I felt completely alone. Damn it. Why couldn't I have been better in that moment?

I ambled over to a corner of my room and tried to reach Yemi. No answer. I tried Almaz next. Straight to voicemail. Seble. Nothing. They were probably tired, busy, or sleeping. I was the only one who had no husband or partner, no present children or grandchildren. It was just me and my thoughts.

I recalled what the doctor had said—about needing

someone who knows my baseline. Someone to speak for me. But what if there was no one who knew the full version of me anymore?

So... I wrote them down. Page after page. I got more organized and more honest. I made progress toward my goal instead of wallowing in pity. There was no time for that anyway.

10

THE BODY REMEMBERS

Two days later, I walked into a dance class with my friends. I decided not to cancel on them again and to make time for enjoyment in my life regardless of everything. I was so glad I did. Instantly, I felt transported to a more beautiful time. Fluid. Free. Not fraught with complexities and overthinking.

The studio was warm and smelled faintly of citrus and sweat. Mirrors lined the walls, distorting us just enough to remind me I wasn't thirty anymore, but not enough to make me care. I knew I still had life in me. The instructor clapped sharply over the music, which ranged from reggaeton to salsa. Her voice high and melodic as she shouted directions in time with the beat.

"Right! Left! Forward and back! Let it *move* through you!"

Seble leaned in, eyes on a man across the room. "He's been drifting this way since the warm-up."

Almaz didn't look. "Maybe he likes a challenge."

Yemi grinned. "Or maybe he's just hoping one of us is bored. Ha! Not a chance." She shimmied her hips to the beat and tossed her head in exuberant abandon. Her hair whipped about as she moved.

It felt good to be out with my sisters.

I let their banter carry me as the rhythm took over. Shoulders, hips, feet. My arms arched instinctively with the music, and I caught my reflection mid-turn. The shimmer of sweat at my temple made me smile. I still had it. Maybe not all of it, but enough. I was careful not to go too fast—didn't want to lose my balance, but I did not let pain and stiffness stop me.

Halfway through the second combination, I found myself partnered with a tall and broad stranger. Probably ex-military based on the posture. He smiled but didn't speak, letting the Latin sounds guide us. His palm at my back was steady but respectful. I let myself follow but it only took seconds for Ezra to flicker across my thoughts. The way he left. The way he wouldn't tell me the truth. Why couldn't I let that go?

The song ended, and applause broke out. A few people grabbed water. I walked toward my tote, catching my breath and trying to shake off my thoughts to remain present. That's when a young woman near the mirrors caught my eye. She sported a short bob, orange and green UM tank top, and was all smiles. Her timing had been sharp the whole class. She caught me watching during the next turn.

"Nice lines," she said, not stopping. "Your left foot leads strong."

I laughed under my breath. "I'll take it."

We moved into a new sequence. She kept pace, still close.

"I'm Mae," I said between breaths.

"Kendra." She smiled warmly.

The instructor shouted another shift and clapped her hands overhead.

"I like this place," I offered.

Kendra nodded. "Good light. Solid playlist. I come here straight from court most days—my job—it wrings the nonsense out."

Before I could ask anything else, she spun away with the next rotation and disappeared back into the rhythm like she'd always belonged there. Fatigue was catching up to me now. And I needed water. The music pulsed louder, but I decided to take a break and watch Almaz, Seble and Yemi continue enjoying themselves. Thoughts of Ezra, Kai, my hands—they all pressed in and slipped away again. The body remembers. But it also knows how to rewrite itself. I got up and rejoined the group, moving through the chorus with my chest open. Sweat clung under my arms. My breath shortened, but I welcomed the ache. It was at least tied to something fun.

The music changed again—something deeper, slower, with drums I could feel in my belly. The instructor dimmed the lights.

"Last round," she told us. "I want you to move like no one's watching. No choreography. Just you and the floor."

Kendra was already mid-spiral and barefoot now. Seble lifted her arms like wings. Almaz closed her eyes and moved from her center. And me? I *danced*. Because I could! I was going to hit the bed hard that night. I knew it.

NORMAL LIFE quickly crept back in once I left. So did the pressure of everything I'd pushed aside. I knew I needed to apologize to Ezra, but I couldn't bring myself to do it yet. I was exhausted. Plus, on the way out, I'd invited the girls over for lunch the next day. Totally unplanned yet it felt right.

The get-together was nothing fancy—just injera, grilled vegetables, and too many dips. I'd even lit a candle. Upbeat music played low to drown out my thoughts.

They arrived late and out of order, the way they always had. Yemi came first, with arms full of flowers. Seble walked in last, wearing sunglasses indoors and sipping from her thermos.

"Lililililili!" Almaz followed ten minutes later with a shrill ululation and store-bought cookies, plus her usual apology for not having time to bake.

Yemi's shoulders twitched, a half-hearted Eskista shimmy she would look amazing doing if she'd followed through. Twenty years of friendship, and Almaz's howls still rewired Yemi's dance reflexes.

It hadn't even been twenty-four hours since I'd seen them, but I still missed their noise.

"You lit a candle?" Seble asked. She pulled off her sunglasses and hooked them into her collar like a librarian marking her page. "Is this a séance or another confession?"

"I was aiming for 'intentional hosting,'" I retorted.

"Intentional hosting," Yemi repeated with mock reverence. "Heh! Somebody's been reading a self-help book!"

Almaz grabbed Seble's thermos for a taste. "Ai! This is just... tea?"

"What did you think it was, katikala? Eh? The village moonshine?"

We all shrugged as Almaz verbalized our thoughts. "With you? Always."

"Eh, Makeda, this injera is older than my grudges. And yet," she took a bite. "It is still perfect. Soft in the middle, like you."

We settled into the living room, and they moved like they'd never left. I brought out tea, even though the day was warm. We were all old-school in different ways. After the initial recap of the night before, I cleared my throat. "I asked you here because I need help."

A collective gasp. "Are you pregnant?"

"Seble!" I laughed even though I didn't want to. "Can I continue, please?" The room reluctantly quieted.

Three heads turned toward me. Yemi's smile softened. Almaz leaned forward slightly, which for her counted as serious concern. Seble raised a brow but said nothing.

"Not the dramatic kind," I added. "I'm not dying, and I don't need any casseroles."

"You better not," Seble muttered. "Because I didn't bring any cheese, old woman!"

"Says the lady who still uses a thermos like it's 1982!" I fired back.

"And Key West is in just a few weeks!"

I let out a small laugh. "It's more like—I need structure. I've been writing something. A memoir. Or essay collection.

I'm not sure yet. The kind that says: I lived. I mattered. I was here."

They all smiled.

"You told me it was an essay," Yemi cut in. "Everyone, the other day Mae promised to read an excerpt from her new book on the trip."

"Well, well, well!

"So, what do you need from us?" Almaz quizzed.

"Well..." the truth was I hadn't fully thought this request through before it fell from my lips, so I said what made the most sense in the moment. "Deadlines. Reminders. Annoyance, if necessary."

"Annoyance," Almaz repeated, reaching for another cookie. "That I can do. Should we start a group chat with threats?"

"How about Bible verses at 3 AM?" Seble ratcheted the moment up.

"I'm being serious."

"So are we." Yemi's voice was calm. "You're finally talking about yourself, and we are not letting you slip out of it! It's about time, Makeda."

I felt seen. Not exposed, but maybe *held* in that moment. "I also might need some physical help," I continued. My nerves were worming their way up my neck, but I knew I had to continue. "My hands...they're not always what they used to be. And my walk isn't always steady despite the show I put on last night," I paused again. "I might need a ride to therapy sometimes."

"Without question!"

"Of course."

"Anything you need, Makeda. You know this."

There was a beat. I felt so relieved and loved. And then Almaz tilted her head at me. "There's something else."

"What do you mean?"

"You're softer lately. Not weak or anything. Just...not always armoring up." She narrowed her eyes. "Is there a man?"

I gulped. Blinked.

Seble perked up like someone had just flipped a switch. "That would explain the candle."

"Oh, please, I have enough candles to be considered a witch!" I laughed, but didn't deny the man part. "There is someone. His name is Ezra, and he's a locksmith. A bit younger than me but—"

Yemi sucked her teeth. "That sounds made up."

"It's not! I called him to help me open an old box and well...we stayed in touch. He's kind. Smart. Charming in a way that doesn't try too hard. We've spent time together."

"You slept with him," Seble said flatly.

"Allah, no!" I answered. "It wasn't like that. We had a beautiful night. Gardens. Drinks. Slow talk. And then something happened that knocked the wind out of me."

I told them about Luther, and my revealing that to Ezra. The tension. The shutting down. The walking out. And that I had not called him since.

"I didn't think it would be such a big deal although I knew better than to push him to talk about family matters before he was ready. Me, of all people, knows better!" I genuinely missed his company, I realized, in that very moment.

Yemi winced. "That's a lot."

"I know."

"Do you want to see him again?" Almaz asked.

I took a breath. "Yes. But not to fix anything. I don't want another project. I want honesty. If he can't meet me there, then no." I didn't know how much I meant the last part in my current state, given I'd need to be just as honest with him, which meant meeting my familial demons as well.

Seble stretched her legs and crossed them again. "Look at you. Talking about memoirs and men in the same breath. We might actually get a new version of you this year. He heeeee!"

"Let's not name her yet," I giggled. "She's still adjusting."

But they were right. Something had shifted. I was still in the thick of it.

We talked more—about other things. Grandchildren. Travel. Staying on top of my health—and theirs, too. I wasn't the only one managing my body in unexpected ways due to age. We also chatted about the price of good olives, and if we should do a 'girls trip' back to Ethiopia one day. The air between us had altered in a beautiful way that didn't feel temporary to that afternoon. It was a renewal.

"Makeda, call the man if you want him around," Almaz ended our get together as they walked out.

"True. True. There's no time for regrets or miscommunication now, friend. If you want him, go after him. Then see how you feel after things are clearer, eh?" Yemi added.

I nodded. They were right.

Later that evening when the dishes were clean and stacked for drying, I sat down to journal but didn't. My pen rested just above the blank page, ink waiting. I was stalling the call. Eventually, I jotted down some chapter title ideas based on all of the notes I'd already written. A collection of essays, I'd also decided. That's what my book would be. They came out as:

Silence is a Heavy Inheritance
In Case I'm Ever Misremembered
What I Unlearned to Survive
Before the Diagnosis Had a Name
On Thursdays, I Was Brave
Some Stories Aren't Meant to Be Useful
The First Time I Swallowed Myself Whole
The Sound of Landing
Notes for the Daughter I Never Had
The Son Who Chose to Forget Me
How to Stand in a Room Without Disappearing

I stared at the list—a fleeting memory of the shampoo Alex used as a boy wafted through when I wrote the second-to-last title. The blue bottle with the yellow duck logo. His soft brown curls, damp and fragrant, and those beautiful blue eyes. I exhaled. My chest didn't ache so much as it folded inward. I didn't know if I could write about all of this, but my mind was clearly pulling the memories and already trying. It was a start. A deep sigh escaped me as I sat back, looking at the ceiling. *Tell it all*, I heard my inner voice and gulped.

"GRIEF AND GRATITUDE are holding hands again." I scribbled the words down and said them aloud. I let my chest rise and fall without urgency. Just embodying the breath and the cycle of emotions that spread through my body. The earlier reset with my girlfriends came back to me like a pulse. I needed that. Nothing could ever replace those women in my life. The laughter had faded, but it left fresh fingerprints on my heart.

Before my friends, I had a habit of "being strong" alone for too long. And when you move through life like that, you realize there's no one to check if the scaffolding's rotting underneath. Including yourself, which is why they meant so much to me. Still, I also needed something else. To clean up the quiet mess I'd made with Ezra. I didn't miss him like a teenager misses a crush, but I did miss the way I felt in his presence—steadied but still free to float. So...I did the necessary.

I picked up my phone and called him. It rang twice before it went to voicemail. My nostrils flared, but I didn't hang up. I hesitated only a moment, then spoke: "Hi. It's Mae. I'm sorry about the other day...I just wanted to say I understand. Family wounds are personal, and I spoke into something that wasn't my place. I recognize that, and take responsibility. But...I also like being around you. That night in the garden wasn't nothing to me. I apologize. I would really like to see you again. If that's something you still want."

Pause.

"I hope you're well. That's all."

I hung up, set the phone down, then exhaled again. The last line was terrible. What was this – corporate? But I couldn't take it back now.

I'd just started climbing in bed when my phone buzzed. *Ezra.* I smiled at the screen, then answered.

"Hey." His voice was soft and tender. "Thank you for the message."

I leaned against the wall. "You're welcome."

"I also didn't handle things well. I'm not used to being seen that clearly. It startled me. I'm sorry too."

"We all startle when the light hits us just right."

A silence.

"Can I see you tomorrow?" he queried.

"Absolutely." I didn't hesitate.

"I'll bring something sweet. You pick the place."

"I think I need to be watching my sugar," I said, grinning. "But I'll make an exception...especially for you."

"And you're all the sugar I need, Mae!"

THE NEXT DAY we met at Dania Beach just before sunset. It was more crowded than I expected, with a mix of families, couples, and lone walkers with headphones. Every now and then, however, you could see planes taking off over the ocean from the nearby Ft. Lauderdale airport. It was so peaceful and dreamy to witness. I didn't live anywhere near this beach, but I always adored how unique it was.

Ezra was already there, waiting near the pier with a blanket slung over one shoulder, cupcakes in one hand and his shoes in the other.

"You were serious about the sugar swap," I grinned.

He smiled. "These don't come with regrets. Usually."

We walked for a while without filling the space. Just letting the wind thread between us and sand cling to our toes. I noticed him glance at my wrist once—my tremor was visible. It felt like a soft percussion under my skin.

"You okay, Mae?"

"Yeah, uh...it's just a new condition I'm getting used to," I told the truth. "I'm fine."

When we reached a quieter stretch, he lay the blanket down, but neither of us sat right away.

"I used to love being near the water. Back when Ethiopia still touched the Red Sea, those beaches were stunning," I remembered aloud. "The waters were turquoise and quiet... almost too perfect," I smiled. "Then you'd see a line of goats or a camel picking its way across the shore like it wandered out of the wrong story."

"Goats at the beach?" Ezra was astonished.

I chuckled. "Yes, believe it or not. I grew up swimming in the Red Sea, watching the sunset with my family and a caravan of camels."

"Wow. Honestly, I'm terrible at geography. Didn't even know Ethiopia was on a coast."

"Well, it isn't anymore. That's a history lesson for another day if you're still curious," I smiled. "But it's close enough to Somalia and Djibouti, which are on the East African coast."

"Got it."

He studied me, careful not to crowd.

"Something about the water always made me feel so at home in my body."

"I don't go in much these days," I stared at the Florida horizon, bringing myself to the present.

Ezra stepped forward and let the tide run over his large feet. "You want to?"

"Well...I'm not exactly dressed for it."

"Oh, Mae. You don't need to be!" Ezra looked at me like a teenager with a dare.

Why not? I thought, then I kicked off my sandals. I pulled my scarf loose and peeled off my top, leaving just my tank and linen pants on.

"Yeah, that's it!" Ezra egged me on.

I couldn't believe I was going to do this! Each step toward the water made me feel younger. Sillier. Freer. I walked in. "Whew!" The ocean was cool but not too much to undermine my gleeful return to it.

Ezra immediately followed, stripping down to his shorts. That's when I got proof that his body was still a bit hard under all of those clothes. Very nice. When I waded deeper, the sea cupped the small of my back and pressed gently at my thighs. I felt my own shape again. Here. Now. Not in the mirror. Not in memory. And it was incredible.

"Oh, my goodness..." I heard myself moan under my breath. Instantly, I felt so good.

Ezra dunked his head under and came up grinning. "You were holding out on me. You're a water woman."

"I'm a *grown* woman!" I shot back, flicking droplets toward his dark chest. A small patch of salt and pepper hairs now wet lay in a beautiful mess against it.

"Oh, we're doing that, now, huh?" he laughed, then splashed me harder.

I gasped and shielded my face. "Careful! These earrings are older than you."

"That just makes 'em vintage, like you, Mae. And valuable." He winked and dipped under again, emerging near me. "I'll be careful. But keep living with me!"

I moved away just enough to keep control, but close enough to make him wonder. "This isn't a baptism," I yelled, catching my breath. "No need to dunk me."

Ezra circled to my side, just waist-deep now. "No. I'm not here with religion to save you. Just to see if you still float."

"Oh, I float on my back," I flirted. And just like that, young Makeda's spirit came out. "I just don't always let people watch. **But...I know how to give you something worth seeing.**"

He blinked, a little stunned. "I should've brought binoculars."

"Oh?"

He swam closer, the water breaking around his shoulders. "Yeah. So, I don't miss an inch of what you might show me."

His words warmed me. The water cooled everything but that. My body and soul felt free. This evening was perfect. Ezra held my gaze for several seconds after his last statement. I could feel his hand meet mine under the flow. The touch made me exhale and smile. Nothing in me was stiff or in pain in that moment.

We let the waves sway us in and out. The sky darkened into lavender and gold. We played a bit more, and I tilted my head back and laughed—deep, chest-first, joyful. Ezra chuckled too, softer.

Then I flicked water at him again, harder this time. "That's for leaving without saying goodbye the other night."

He blinked. "I thought we weren't doing that part right now."

"We're not," I said. "But I still get to splash you."

"Fair."

He caught my hand once, briefly. Then let it go. A pause. A beat between waves.

"I missed this," I vocalized.

"The beach?"

"No," I said, letting my fingers skim the surface. "Me."

Eventually, we drifted out of the water, skin damp and feet heavy with sand. Ezra handed me the edge of the blanket. I sat first, pulling my knees toward my chest. My tank clung to me.

He opened the box. "Cupcake truce?"

I took one. Coconut with a glossy dollop of icing. "Truce."

We ate in comfortable silence, both a little breathless. The wind played with the edge of my scarf where I'd draped it over my shoulder again. Ezra adjusted it slightly, then let his hand drop to my back.

"You know," he began, "for someone who says she's not spontaneous—you're better at it than most."

"Thank you." I smiled, big, and full of pride. Ezra's affirmation made my bones remember pure joy.

We took turns writing our names in the sand after eating as the tide rolled in again ahead of us. Planes continued blinking silently overhead. Someone a few yards down lit a small sparkler, and it fizzed gold into the twilight before dying out.

I leaned back on my elbows. "I really appreciate this moment, Ezra. That water really woke something up."

Ezra lay beside me, not touching, just there. "Good. Let's not put you back to sleep."

ON THE MORNING AFTER, Ezra and I met at a community event where Kai was performing. We hadn't planned to spend so much time together so soon, but after the beach we'd talked almost all night and he convinced me to allow him into my plans for the next day.

The event had a great turnout. Folding chairs fanned out in uneven rows, most already claimed. The air inside buzzed with the scent of coffee and cinnamon bread. With sweat and anticipation. Kai spotted me and waved from the front. She had a notebook in one hand and a mic in the other.

Ezra appeared beside me with glee. His energy was incredibly calming.

"You made it," I acknowledged.

"I told you I would." He beamed. "Besides, I wanted to hear the kid who convinced you to write a book."

I'd told him more about my plans and who had helped solidify the idea. Told him I'd wanted the book done and published in the next six months, and he promised to "hold me to it."

Kai was performing poetry today, and she was up third. Sharp, fast, delivered with the uneven rhythm of someone still learning breath control, her words were defiantly strong. The piece was about silence. Her mother's silence. Her aunt's rage. Her own refusal to inherit the hush. The room held its breath for her.

When it ended, someone near us asked, "Is that the girl you've been mentoring?"

I shook my head without fully looking to see who had called out. "She's the one who's been mentoring me."

Ezra looked over. His eyes widened. It was Luther.

I could tell from his gait and Ezra's instant seizing up beside me. Luther still had shades on even though we were inside. He came closer. Ezra was no longer relaxed. He shuffled his feet.

"Well, well," Luther sang as he reached us. "Didn't expect to see you here. What's this—a date?"

His voice wasn't loud, but the tone cut.

"Luther...right?" I greeted. Neutral. I didn't really *know* this man.

Ezra's jaw flexed. "What do you want, man?"

Luther ignored him and looked straight at me.

"You're even more beautiful than the other day," he complimented. Or taunted?

I was confused. I didn't answer.

"You've still got good taste, brother," he turned to Ezra, and then back at me. "But be careful," he told me. "This one is good at selling ease and a good time. Makes it look like peace when it's just resentment."

What?

"Knock it off, bro!" Ezra was aggravated but restrained.

But Luther kept going.

"Funny, seeing him here. Supporting something. Someone. I only know him to disappear when things matter."

I gasped.

"You didn't even tell her, did you?" Luther glanced at his

brother. "You brought her here playing the stable man routine and didn't even mention how you burned the last bridge you had?"

Ezra turned slightly. Not toward Luther, but away from me. "I don't owe you my story, man."

Luther smirked. "No, but I'm still in it. And that eats you alive."

That landed. Ezra stepped back.

I cut in. "I don't know what either of you are performing right now, but I did not agree to be an audience."

Luther looked at me, and for the first time, something flickered in his face. Ego. "Welp, I didn't mean to interrupt," he teased. "Just thought I'd say hello to my brother and his new prize, I suppose. You just look so happy together. I hope it lasts." And with that, he turned and walked away.

Ezra stood like stone.

"Let's get some air." I suggested, and we left without another word.

Outside, Ezra lit a cigarette. I hated the smell, but I'd sensed worse from men in darker places with harder truths. He didn't speak. I didn't ask. I knew I said I wanted honesty, just not always in the moment it demands the highest cost. Timing mattered with deep emotions, that much I knew deeply. Whatever Luther stirred up, I'd ask about it later. I wasn't carrying it before I had to.

11

OPAL & VINE

Ezra was trying too hard to look calm, and that's how I knew he wasn't. He still hadn't told me what stirred behind that cigarette after the run-in with Luther, but tonight wasn't the night to ruin with a damper of old family drama. Soon, though. I would ask him about it soon. Tonight, though, we were on a more refined date—someplace Ezra was eager to show me because he'd had a part in designing somehow.

The evening was gorgeous—finally not too hot, and here he was, smoothing his collar and mumbling about the humidity while a valet opened my door. The hem of my dress eagerly caught the night breeze, and its cinnamon silk cut just below the knee. My garb's sleeves kissed my elbows and had a neckline that said *look if you want, but you'll never know everything. I felt incredible, gliding in a* color that matched the inside of a ripe fig.

"This place uses two kinds of stone," Ezra announced

when he made his way to my side. "I helped build the wine vault design years ago. Didn't expect it to get this... flashy."

"It's just fine, Ezra." I secured my lacquered clutch from Dakar. It had a small chip on the corner, but I wouldn't dare throw it out because of such a minor imperfection. I nudged Ezra forward.

We were on our third date now, and despite a few unspoken words, things were going lovely.

"Love the paint on that bag," he complimented.

"Thank you."

"The whole ensemble, really. You're so...different, Mae. I love it!"

Inside the restaurant *Opal & Vine*, everything was polished and moneyed. Every woman looked expensive and chill. Even the furniture had manners. The lighting was that soft kind that made everything look filtered in real-time. This was a gigantic difference from what Ezra and I had experienced so far. But he leveled up and looked good in his jacket and tie.

For a split second, *I* felt like a thread out of place. Like my shoes were too worn, or like I was the only one here who remembered sweat. But then Ezra placed his hand low on my back and said, "Mae, this room's been waiting for someone to show it how it's done."

And just like that, I remembered who I was.

A violinist played near the bar. His music was so delicate.

"It's like he's trying not to offend the silverware," I giggled to Ezra.

He chuckled before saying my name low and close. "There," he nodded toward a glass wall next to a stunning wine display. "That's my work! The vault is climate-sealed with no visible locks. The shelves are weight-balanced and everything," he grinned. "It took me six prototypes to get the airflow right."

I followed his gaze. It was beautiful, I had to admit. Quietly clever just like him. "Have you ever shown it to anyone else?" I watched the violet LED strips highlight the wine labels like jewelry.

"No. Just you," he beamed.

The maître d' greeted us with a small bow. "Table eight."

We followed him to a space beneath a small chandelier where I sat, conscious of how much light hit the back of my hands. They looked older tonight.

Birthday toasts and various conversations filled the room as Ezra and I chatted about everything we could think of during the first hour. Somewhere near the front, the violinist paused, then picked up again—this time with something sweeter. More romantic.

I lifted my water glass and with a mindless glance around the restaurant, my eyes landed on him.

Alex.

There, near the entrance. Straight spine, tailored suit, that magazine-spread smile that never quite felt heartfelt. He looked like a press release.

I froze. Fork halfway to my mouth.

Ezra noticed.

"What's wrong?"

I didn't answer right away. I watched the young woman next to Alex instead. Pretty girl—the same one from the news clipping I'd seen—in a white cocktail dress and gorgeous updo. Wrong kind of stillness in her shoulders, though, and her hand kept drifting to her necklace then back to her lap once they sat down.

"That...that's my son," I confessed.

Ezra's eyes widened before turning subtly to look. Then back at me. "The one you haven't spoken to?"

Yes.

Ezra slumped. "Do you want to wrap things up and leave?" he offered. "If you're uncomfortable, Mae—"

"No," I said, too quickly. "He doesn't even know I'm here."

The maître d' floated past with a wine list we didn't need. I waved him off. My mouth was too dry for wine.

From where I sat, I couldn't hear the words, but I could see that Alex's gestures were heavily rehearsed. The way he leaned in with exactly the right amount of intensity, the soft reach for her hand, the dramatic pause before signaling the sommelier. He'd always known how to choreograph a moment. Even when he was a boy, he practiced his smiles in the mirror. I used to think that was sweet. Now I knew better. Alex *needed* this night to be perfect.

"So, you never met his girlfriend?" Ezra wondered aloud.

"No," I mumbled. "Though he did recently call out-of-the-blue, we didn't really talk. We haven't had a real conversation in decades."

"Oh my..."

I watched her more than I watched Alex while Ezra looked at me. The musician shifted songs, and Alex stood. His chair scraped softly against the marble, and the lighting caught his face just right. He reached into his jacket pocket and dropped something on the floor. The woman noticed, but kept focused on his movements. He reached for her hand and my heart skipped. I could feel Ezra's eyes piercing me even more now, but I had no words. What could I say? What could I even do besides maintain control—or at least a semblance of it?

The ring appeared, and the room inhaled like one organism. All those strangers wanted the same fairy tale at the same time, and for one shard of a second, I felt the pride no mother forfeits—my boy, taller than everything, asking for forever.

"Mae?" Ezra tried me again. His voice brought me back to the present. Back to the truth. Back to hurt.

I couldn't believe I was witnessing this from a quiet table across the room. My eyes wouldn't let me look away. "She doesn't look sure," I discerned.

Most people didn't notice but I saw it. Years of reading people enabled me to almost hear her bones whispering, *This isn't what we asked for.* And still, she said yes. Of course she did. Who can say no with that many eyes on them—as the star of such a grand gesture and scene?

"Are you going to speak to him?" Ezra interrupted my thoughts. "You can't just let him abandon you like this. It's not normal. It's not okay. It's insane, Mae, to witness this from across the room like an old ghost."

I almost couldn't believe his defense of me. So passionate. But still, I wondered aloud, "Don't you have a brother you don't talk to?"

Ezra blinked. Ouch.

I hadn't planned to say that, but it came out effortlessly. Hell, I felt bad about it even though it was a legitimate question. Bad timing. But...maybe I didn't just want Ezra to speak to his brother because it was the "right thing to do," but because I wanted someone else to go first. To show me how to survive being left and still say yes when the door opens again.

Applause rolled through the dining room like a chainsaw through tension. Everything sounded, felt, and sat differently with me. Ezra's hand grazed mine on the table but didn't push. He knew better. My spine had gone straight as a ruler. Alex helped his fiancée up and champagne was poured. My feet bounced ridiculously under the table as I watched them kiss. He scanned the room to savor the adulation. A nod here. A smile there. But he never saw me. That was the part that hit me like a stone in the chest—he wasn't hiding from me. I wasn't on his radar at all.

"Check please." Ezra didn't wait for permission anymore.

I didn't cry. That would've made it about me, and it wasn't. But I felt it in my hands—stiff, heavy, old. I felt it in the way my teeth clenched. In the tiny pinch behind my left eye. At this point, I just wanted to leave before the engagement ring caught the light again.

"Thanks," I whispered, grateful Ezra took the lead at the right time. "I do need to go now. I'm sorry."

"Never apologize for your needs, Mae."

The valet line was slow-moving outside. I stood there, arms crossed, trying not to feel like an apparition. As if the night hadn't been enough, I couldn't believe that the next few moments would have Alex less than 20 feet away from me, with his tailored suit, proud smile, and piercing blue eyes, just like his father – but without the grace, love, and empathy. He'd just exited with his fiancée—her hand still loosely in his.

"Congratulations, guys!" Folks still sent them well-wishes.

Alex's smile was wide like a mountain. He'd conquered the evening and gotten the yes he wanted. But then his eyes caught mine. And everything stopped. His whole body went still. Just the widening of his eyes—like saucers—and a deep furrowing of his brows. Meanwhile, a fat tear forced its way into my eye.

We held the stare. No words. No gestures. But the single tear rolled down my cheek at this silent crossing as I watched his lips part in shock. I didn't have the strength to stop the wail of my soul anymore, though it was still quiet for now. The valet called a number, and Ezra's hand brushed mine, grounding me. Alex didn't move at first, but he eventually turned away before our car pulled up. My heart shattered, and my entire body shook as the valet opened the car door and Ezra slipped into the driver's seat.

Inside was when I broke. It started low. A shift in my breath and a grip of the door handle. Then the sting behind the eyes. A rattle I couldn't blame on Parkinson's. My soul was gurgling, and I bent forward at the waist, elbows on knees, hands locked together like I could hold myself upright if I gripped hard enough.

"Why? I don't understand!"

Ezra pulled out of the line with one hand on my knee. "Mae?"

"Damn it. Damn it. Damn it!" Hot tears rolled down my

cheeks for the grief and the rage. For the swelling curiosity of not knowing *why* my son hated me so much. "I'm so tired. So Goddamned tired!"

Ezra turned onto Hallandale Beach Boulevard and drove in silence. I knew he didn't know what to say. I didn't even think there was anything he *could* say to make me feel better. He kept his hand on my leg—with only a slight squeeze now and then in lieu of words—and let me release. A few minutes later, he pulled into a small overlook facing the Intracoastal.

"I'm gonna stop here," he said quietly. The water was wide and dark. It stirred only by a passing boat.

Parked and with the engine now off. The evening was deafening until I broke through it. "I don't know what I did." My voice cracked. "We were close, and then we weren't. After my divorce, I expected some fallout. Moving away—sure, there'd be friction. But with Alex, it wasn't an explosion. It was slow."

"He started to pull back despite his father and me co-parenting from a distance. It was too much for Alex to be away from him most of the time, I guess. I don't know. But I...I let him withdraw more and more as he got older."

Ezra turned toward me slightly. His chest heaved up and down in a big exhale as he listened.

"I fed him. I paid attention. Paid for his study abroad trips to Europe and worked with his dad to ensure he got through college and business school. But," I paused as the truth started to ignite at my lips.

"But what?"

"I, um...I dunno."

"Mae?"

"What, Ezra?!"

He inched back. Gulped.

I huffed. "I also—I think I taught him to hold things in and to leave when it hurts." I paused. The next words came out like blood. "I am the one who always insisted everything be perfect. It was how I'd learn to minimize aggressions when I landed in the States—and eventually dating a white man. Even though I genuinely loved his father," I looked down, "Part of it was strategic in the beginning." Shame. It washed over me like a tidal wave. I'd never admitted that part aloud.

Ezra said nothing.

"But then I initiated the dissolution of our 'perfect' family and moved him across state lines while calling it a fresh start." I exhaled hard. My head ached. "But I never asked what it felt like for him. I assumed he was okay because we didn't scream in each other's faces. We had dinner. I showed up. I thought that meant we were fine."

A beat.

"Maybe he thought I was a hypocrite for honoring Ethiopia in our home but raising white presentation to have more value. Maybe my ability to close off emotionally was just masking grief with structure and he saw through it. Maybe disappearing runs in my blood. Countries. Names. People. I don't know. I just never thought I'd be the only one left."

Ezra put his arms around me, but still remained quiet. I needed that.

"I trained him to keep going. To always *win*. To get over it instead of through it. So, when I shattered the image, maybe he just filed me under 'flawed' and moved on."

"Oh, Mae." Ezra groaned.

My hands juddered in my lap.

"Don't be so hard on yourself. It all can't be your fault."

"I used to think silence meant resilience. But I guess he learned silence meant erasure."

"But you didn't stop loving him."

"Never. No," I confirmed. "But I made it easier for him not to need it."

"That's a heavy load to carry, Mae."

"Someone has to though. Someone has to take responsibility for this fracture."

"I mean..." Ezra couldn't find the words.

"And I didn't know how to hold his whiteness," I added—another confession for the first time in my life. "I loved all of him, but I don't think I made space for the parts of him that didn't come from me."

That truth nearly undid me.

"He learned to disappear by watching me, and now I'm furious he got so good at it."

The tears came again. More like a river's stream this time. It was like something unscrewed from deep inside of me and just let decades of it go.

"I'm sorry, Mae. I know that doesn't mean much, but I hate to see you hurting like this. I wish I could do something, but I know I can't." He breathed slowly. Staying.

I'd said more to Ezra than I'd ever said to anyone else, not even my closest girlfriends or myself. And that—that was enough—him being a safe space. I tossed my head back against the headrest in the quiet. Now both of us were quiet and looked out at the night. A clearing breeze pushed through our half-down windows, cooling the moment. So much for this being a wonderful date. Maybe an honest night was better than a wonderful one even though it hurt like hell.

Eventually, Ezra merged us back onto the road. Just as he pulled in front of my building he spoke again. "Mae, there's something I should have said the other day."

"I can't. I'm sorry. I want to know, I do. But I can't tonight. I am at emotional capacity. I'm sorry."

"No need. I should have known better."

Ezra looked deeply into my eyes and cupped my face with his hand. He rubbed his thumb over my chin while putting his other hand back on my leg. "I'm sorry tonight turned out the way it did. I really...really wanted it to be special but—"

"It's not your fault at all. Thank you for holding space for me."

"It was my honor, Mae. Get some rest tonight, please."

"I will." I touched the hand he had on my face. Nuzzled my lips against his fingertips and then opened the car door. "Good night, Ezra. I'll call you."

"Good night."

12

THE CUT LINE

My stomach growled loudly the next morning. I didn't eat right away. I didn't stretch or open the curtains either. I just sat at the table with my coffee and a swarm of thoughts buzzing in my brain. Scattered pages faced me. Scribbles. Phrases. Mismatched paragraphs and margin notes in red ink. A few words about the first time I saw Alex in a sonogram image with Robert by my side. A line about my father lighting a cigarette instead of saying goodbye. I'd circled both three times and still hadn't used either. I pushed everything aside but one clean sheet. Today, I would finish essay one: *Silence is a Heavy Inheritance.*

I set a timer on my phone and challenged myself to write in a sprint. I wrote until my fingers cramped and my tongue felt dry even though I wasn't speaking. What came out was untidy and didn't follow the format I used to teach, but it was true and that's all I cared about.

I stared at the final sentence when I finished, then pressed my clammy hands against the table. Instead of reading it right away, I got up and poured the coffee I never drank down the sink.

"I need to type this up and print it out," I mumbled to myself. I knew it was an extra step to write it by hand first, but it felt more real that way.

"I will read this in Key West."

Then my phone rang from a blocked number. I almost let it go to voicemail, but something in my chest pulled tight and I knew. I answered.

"Mother?" came the voice. Controlled. Low. Cautious.

I sat. "Alex."

A fat silence.

"You called me first," I said, too stubborn to be more welcoming. "So, I assume you want something."

"I wasn't sure you'd answer."

"Well. I did."

He hesitated. "I've been thinking about... things. I'm getting married and..."

There it was.

"I know. I saw your eng—"

"I know. About that—"

"I haven't heard from you in more than fifteen years, Alex, and we live in the same city."

I had to stand up to release the swell of energy rising up my legs. I paced out to my balcony and then back inside before standing with my back to the window. His silence squatted in my ear like nuisance static. Faint traffic passed on his end. A dog barked twice on mine, then nothing.

He didn't ask how I was. Didn't say why he was calling now.

"You could've looked me up. Slipped a note under the door. Son, you could've shouted my name at a crosswalk," I breathed. "But you waited until there was a ring on that woman's finger. A woman I've never even met and who likely doesn't know I exist." *And one who didn't look as if she was sure she wanted to marry you*, I thought, but didn't say.

"It's not about that," he defended.

"No?"

"No," he exhaled. "I just...I don't know. How—how have you been? I didn't plan this, you know?" he rambled. "I saw your name somewhere. Maybe on something about an exhibit, and it brought things back. Then I saw you at Opal & Vine..."

Things.

"Memories," he clarified, softly.

I turned from the window. Pushed the stool out from a table with my foot and sat again. "Turn your camera on."

"What?" He sounded incredulous.

"I want to see you."

"That's not—"

"I haven't seen your face up close since you were in your twenties. Don't hide behind this call."

A pause. Then a sigh. I heard the soft click of his screen shifting.

His face appeared. Alex was older and sharper. The boyish fullness in his cheeks had given way to clean angles and a chiseled jawline. The skin beneath his blue eyes was a shade darker than I remembered, and his hair was shorter than he used to wear it. The coils were tighter now, intentionally sculpted. The beard was new. Neat, like the rest of him. The boy was still very handsome, and I imagined he got a weekly shape-up to ensure he stayed that way.

But the set of his shoulders was rigid. His confidence read practiced rather than genuine, and for all that control, his mouth still had the same slight downturn when he was unsettled.

I knew that mouth.

"You look...good," he said, like it hurt.

"You look steady. I know what it takes to fake that."

His jaw set. "I didn't call to fight."

"Then why did you?"

A beat. Then, quietly: "Because I let this distance go on for too long. This lie that I am fine without you and Pop. I mean, I am, but it shouldn't be like this. We're all getting older and I'm going to start a family and..." his voice trailed off into selfish reasons for reconnecting.

Nowhere in his deluge of words was an apology. Not even a confession. Just something close enough to sting.

I nodded once. "Well, I am writing about the life you walked away from. About the life I survived. I'm writing my story for a new book."

He glanced offscreen. "I'm not sure I'm ready to know all that."

"You don't have to. But I'm still going to say it."

"That's fair. It's your life."

"So...what did you expect from this? Am I supposed to have been resurrected to all whom you told that I was dead?"

"I never said that, Mother. I never told people you were dead!"

"Oh?" What a ridiculous lie. I knew he did.

"Well, maybe I did right out of college. But not recently. Not now."

"So, your fiancé knows that I live in town?"

"Not exactly. It never came up."

"Not dead then. Just omitted."

"Mother."

"Alex." We held each other's gaze in a standoff.

A voice called his name in the background. Muffled. Female. Was that his lady love? His eyes flicked toward the sound.

"I have to go," Alex hurried.

"You always do, son." The last word was a butterfly beating in my chest.

I watched him hesitate to end the call. "But I'll be back if you let me." Then the screen went black.

"Oh, Lord, Lord, Lord!" I closed my eyes and stretched my jaw until I heard it pop out the tension it had been holding.

Stuffing my phone in my pocket, I grabbed my keys and carelessly slipped into a pair of shoes by the door. I made my way to my car. The Miami heat burned my skin. With the press of a button, my door clicked open.

I had no destination in mind. I just needed to move.

With no music playing and my chest thudding loud enough to count as percussion, I took Biscayne south past the new condos with their glass jaws and manicured planters. My mind reeled as I passed the strip mall where just days ago, I'd had the time of my life dancing with my friends and strangers.

The A/C blew hard. Too cold. I left it on. Let it scrape back the fiery tears that threatened to stain my cheeks again. A red light held me at NW 54th, and a loudly dressed girl crossed the street with a boxed cake in one hand, dragging a balloon by the string in the other. She reminded me of Kai but was a grown woman. I wanted to ask her where the party was. I wanted to go. Didn't matter if it was irrational. Nothing made sense for me. I wanted not to exist at all.

The light turned green. I didn't move. *Keep it together*, I told myself, but was miserably failing. I was a mess. After all I'd been through and seen in my life, this was worse than I expected. It burned.

A horn behind me jolted something loose, and I turned right into the grimy and raw warehouse district. A dog stood sentry behind a fence, nose pressed through the chain link. A few more lights down, I felt compelled to pull into a lot that no one cared about. Grass popped up across the cracked asphalt like ghetto carrot tops. Broken glass glittered in the sun. I cut the engine and sat.

Silence.

I closed my eyes slowly as my body caught up to the shock of it all. My hands rattled against my knees thinking back to his face on my phone screen. My spine felt like a thousand pounds as I recalled Alex's "Mother" and I folded forward, forehead on the wheel.

"Son."

Just that. One word. Felt enormous in my mouth.

A car zipped into the desolate lot. I didn't look up, but reached for my phone to record. Yet I couldn't bring myself to hit the red button. I had nothing. That was the whole problem.

13

OTHER PEOPLE'S KITCHEN

Two days had passed since my drive to nowhere. Two days since the blood of my body circled back like a contraction that was too late to push back in. I'd kept my calls to Ezra brief, although I did tell him the latest development. I thought about dialing Robert, Alex's father, but decided against it. I needed more time to sit alone with this before making it a whole family ordeal. In the meantime, I folded laundry. Rearranged books I hadn't finished. And wrote two more essays for my book.

When Yemi invited me and the girls to her place to finalize Key West details, I said yes without thinking. I needed to be somewhere I wasn't the center of. Somewhere with noise. Any of their homes would do.

Yemi's house always smelled like cardamom, eucalyptus, and hope. Beautifully decorated yet well lived in, it was the kind of place that had hand-woven tablecloths and old rugs that knew generational stories. Traditional photo frames of lineage lined a table and prayer cards leaned against a ceramic dish of keys and loose change.

Her daughter—Leah, maybe—was headed for the door when I arrived. Gorgeous dress. Playful vibe. Good bone structure and appropriate wedges. She offered a polite smile and I returned the best one I could manage.

"I was just leaving," she announced, grabbing her tablet off the dining room table. "I know how sacred this time is for you ladies."

"Oh, stay," I answered before I could help myself.

Yemi raised an eyebrow but said nothing.

Leah paused and flicked her gaze between us. "Really?"

I glanced at Yemi who shrugged.

"Why not?"

Leah seemed happy to remain, sitting at the other end of the couch. Her presence stretched the room in a way I didn't mind.

"Look at us," Seble dropped a bag of skincare minis on the table. "A bunch of seasoned women getting excited over travel-size lotion and sunscreen. Heh!"

"Speak for yourself," Almaz retorted. "I'm excited over the bartender we booked. What's his name again, Yemi?"

"Lazaro," she winked.

"Mom!" Leah's face was flushed.

"Oh, child, I'm still allowed to admire works of art. Your father certainly does the same. Don't think I don't know."

"Young people," Almaz chuckled.

"I'm thirty-six," Leah said as if it made her sound more adult.

"Still a kid," I smiled. "Enjoy it. I know I loved most of my 30s. Maybe a bit too much!"

Laughter rippled, including mine, but it wasn't as hearty and long as it usually was. Yemi noticed and her brow shifted. Seble handed me a glass of wine.

"Everything alright, Makeda?" Almaz asked gently. Her eyes narrowed.

I nodded, then shook my head. "Not yet. But it will be."

They glanced around at each other but decided not to press. That's the thing about old friends—they know when to hold the space and when to crowd it.

Leah stood to stretch, still scrolling something on her phone. "I'll head out so y'all can be messy in peace."

"You don't have to rush," Yemi called, though her eyes warmed with gratitude.

"I do. But thanks for letting me be honorary auntie for a minute!"

Such a beautiful young lady. We watched her leave and heard the door click shut with a softness that gave me permission.

I looked at my friends and told them everything. I had to. About my date with Ezra and what I ultimately witnessed at Opal & Vine. About Alex's call. His face. The way he said "Mother" like the word was vinegar. I didn't spare myself either. I told them how it knocked the breath from my chest. How I wanted to rewind the screen. How I wanted to hang up first yet couldn't. "What if motherhood and that kind of happiness is a door I can't afford to re-open?" I asked, more to myself than them. None of them answered.

Yemi reached for my hand and held it without squeezing.

Almaz exhaled loud enough to stir the candles on the table. "Damn."

Seble shook her head. "After all these years."

I nodded. "He looks good. But hollow."

That sat in the room like a second bottle of wine no one reached for.

"Well," Almaz proclaimed, sitting taller, "you're still going to Key West. We are *not* canceling a damn thing."

"Of course not," I agreed. Besides, I now had three essays written for my book. It is even more important to me now to finish and publish it. I will not have my story distorted."

"That's right!"

"Just remember," Seble added, "he's not the only one who knows how to come back from nowhere."

That made me smile. A real one this time.

LATER THAT NIGHT, I decided to write the first few pages of *The Son Who Chose to Forget Me* and read it aloud. The action was defiant yet affirming. It felt good to be honest. Felt empowering to not hold back. Then, I started wondering how I'd publish my collection when I finished it. The truth was I had no idea how the process worked without an agent or university press behind me. But...I knew who might: Kai. The little firecracker was always experimenting with digital media, quoting podcast stats, and explaining things like Substack and EPUB formatting like it was second nature. Surely, she could explain all of this to me when it was time.

By morning, I was humming—body settled and mood

improved. The house was spotless. I opened the printed Key West itinerary and laid out my clothes—one outfit per line item. Lightweight linen for the gallery crawl. A turquoise caftan with gold stitching for our beach picnic. My strappy sandals still held up, though I packed the walking sneakers just in case. I misted my perfume onto tissue paper and slipped it between the folds of my dresses like my mother taught me.

Finally, I wasn't getting ready for a disaster. I was preparing for pleasure, and it felt damned good! I could not wait to enjoy the water and shenanigans with my friends. And I was ready to read my pages.

I made a quick list of last-minute things: sunscreen, facial wipes, motion sickness bands just in case. I figured I'd stop by the pharmacy before it got too hot. The checkout line was short.

"Here you go, Dr. Bekele! Enjoy your day," the woman behind the counter chirped.

"Thanks so much."

But it was when I reached into my tote to put back my wallet that the small white prescription bag slipped from my grip and tumbled to the floor. I bent slightly, but a brown hand got there first.

"Here, ma'am," the deep voice said.

I froze.

That voice.

I looked up.

There stood Alex, holding my medication. His eyes nosily scanned the label before his face registered anything else. Then his focus shifted from the bottle to me.

He blinked. "Mother?"

A thousand comebacks flashed through me. I chose none. Instead, I took the bag from his hand. "You *read* it?"

"I—yeah. I mean. I saw Bekele. Wasn't expecting that." He extended the bag for me to take. "Is everything um... okay?"

"Not okay, but not the end of the world, either," I told him.

"You look strong. I mean, I wouldn't have guessed anything was wrong."

Such a foolish thing to say. "Of course you wouldn't. Strong gets mistaken for *well* all the time." I stared him directly in the eyes. "Alex, I have Parkinson's disease."

His lips parted and his eyes widened. He took a micro step back. "What?" The word seemed like it crept out on its own.

"I figured if you could read random bags of people's private medicine like nothing, then I can tell you what actually is."

"Mom. Really?"

"Really what?" I didn't know if he wanted me to confirm my condition or if he was questioning my tone.

His brows furrowed and he took a long look at me. "That's... a lot. I didn't mean to find out this way." He fidgeted. "I—I'm sorry." Alex gulped, a flash of regret crossing his face.

I exhaled slowly. Not knowing what to do with him or the moment.

"Are you here with someone? Or...Do you need a ride home?"

"I'm alone, but I'm fine," I told him while watching him shift his weight from one side to the next. "I'm actually going away tomorrow. Key West."

"For fun?"

"For now."

He gave a dry smile. "Uh, okay. So, it's not too bad then? The Parkinson's?"

A scanner beeped from the checkout. Somewhere behind us, a child begged for candy in a whine that pierced the fluorescent quiet. I held off answering. Alex didn't deserve to know more, did he? I had no idea what was right, wrong, selfish, or preservation anymore.

"I just meant it's good you're still doing things. Living your life."

"That's all I can do, son. Keep moving forward. Keep on living." I turned to leave and end the awkwardness, but he spoke again.

"If you need anything while you're away... you can ask. I'm not saying I expect it. Just saying I'll respond." His words were more deliberate this time. "I know a lot of time has passed but...you know. I'm here now."

I paused to feel his words landing on me. "I'll keep that in mind. But being here once isn't the same as staying." My emotions were a tornado again.

He didn't respond. I gave him a final nod before leaving with my tote on my shoulder. The door slid open with a sigh, and the sun was still waiting outside like nothing had happened. By the time I reached home, however, I'd cleared my mind of him. For the time being at least, I let myself enjoy the feel of new clothes—trying on one dress for the trip once more before packing it. I just wanted to feel how my body moved in it, and it felt good. The new moments of peace prompted me to record a new voice note of my progress despite the new challenges arising daily. I also texted Ezra to remind him of my trip timeline and that I'd be in touch daily. I missed him.

Departure Morning – Seble's House, South Miami, 8:02 AM

THE SUV GLINTED in the driveway. Sleek, black, and polished. Seble had backed it in at sunrise, popped the trunk, and left the hatch open. I arrived with a single carry-on, a canvas tote, and a bouquet of sunflowers I'd picked up on the way for Seble's husband to keep in the house while we were gone. Her hubby, Moses, stood barefoot on the walkway with a garden hose in hand.

"These are for you," I said, holding the bouquet like it meant more than it did. Maybe it did.

He chuckled. "What on earth am I supposed to do with these? Put them in Seble's old wine bottles?"

"Eh, eh, it's too early to talk about wine!" Seble called from somewhere inside.

Almaz was already there. She was dressed in a linen set too white for travel and sunglasses large enough to block out the galaxy. The woman was already rearranging the trunk while fussing at Yemi's luggage for being "the size of a jazz band."

"I need options!" Yemi defended, peeling a boiled egg

and already unwrapping snacks from a cooler bag that clearly violated every road-trip rule.

"Options? This is three outfit changes per day," Almaz fired back. "Are you planning a costume drama in the Keys?"

The bickering was familiar and comforting. None of it meant any harm. Just then, Seble emerged from the house holding car keys and a Tupperware of injera.

"Good morning," she called. "Mae, you are riding next to me. Everyone else can chat too much in the backseat."

"Perfect," I beamed. Excitement was already radiating in me. I desperately needed this girls' trip!

The sun was rising fast, warming the pavement and softening the shadows across the bird of paradise plants adorning Seble's garden. A neighbor waved from her porch, and the air smelled like overripe mango and car exhaust.

As I climbed into the passenger seat, I pulled out my phone to see a missed call from Ezra. I texted back: *We're heading out. I'll send a photo from the highway if these women ever let me sit in peace.* I slipped the cellular into the side pocket of the door, but not before Almaz caught a glimpse.

"Oh? Is that Ezra again?" she teased from the back.

"Mind your own notifications," I told her, but my smile gave me away.

"Don't pretend we don't see it," Yemi chimed in. "You were practically humming while locking your door."

"Can't a single woman enjoy a little happiness?" I quipped.

"You should be locking in a LOT of happiness! This is not the time for 'little' anything in life," Almaz added, and they all murmured in agreement.

"Especially not at our age," Yemi piped. "Little happiness, little meals, little men with little—what are we doing that for?"

I gasped.

"Exactly," Seble threw in from the driver's seat. "If it's not big and satisfying, it's a waste of our time and estrogen! Hee heeee!"

"Speak for yourself," Almaz said. "I've still got plenty of both."

We howled the kind of laughter that makes your chest hurt and your eyes water.

And just like that, we were ready! Almaz insisted on starting with an old Amharic playlist that only she could sing along to. Meanwhile, Yemi started passing around mandazi she swore were "still fresh, just firm." The bread was tough, but none of us said it flat out. Politeness was better for the moment.

As we pulled away from the curb, Seble's husband lifted his hand in a slow wave, his belly peeking out from under his t-shirt. One of the grandkids appeared in the doorway, wide-eyed, still in Spiderman pajamas.

"Bring me something, Grammy!" the child called.

Seble waved from the driver's seat. "We'll see if Key West has Wi-Fi and Roblox merch, Sammy!"

I glanced at the others and settled into my seat. "And if we don't come back with at least three stories we can't tell in front of that child, we've done it wrong!"

We hit US-1 with all the windows cracked, the sun dancing off the hood, and our voices rising. Ten minutes in, Almaz was fighting with the Bluetooth to give us a better soundtrack and silence our complaints about her playlist.

"Why is this playlist in alphabetical order?" she snapped at her phone. "Who listens to music by *file name*?"

"Apparently, you," Seble quipped and took a turn like we were in a Fast & Furious spin-off for aunties.

"Ay ay ay! Slow down now! You want to kill us? Yemi held onto the headrest in front of her. "Please. Seble, brake like your bones matter."

"I am braking. The woman ahead of me is driving like she just got baptized and thinks heaven is waiting."

"Well, Jesus, be a seatbelt!" I snorted.

"You could say 'excuse me' instead of making me drop the peanuts all over the seat," Almaz pouted, brushing snacks off her lap. "This car smells like roasted kernels and regret now."

"I thought I asked you not to open anything until we hit the bridge!" I called over my shoulder, shaking my head at myself for believing they would actually honor my request.

Almaz chirped in mock offense, "If you wanted peace, you should've taken a silent retreat. I am hungry *now*."

Out the window and into the Keys, we passed a pastel-pink gas station shaped like a giant shell. An old tourist trap promising *Live Alligators & Airbrushed T-Shirts was a few doors down.*

"All jokes aside, girls. Thanks so much for organizing this trip," I vocalized as a sea of palm trees blurred into the distance and the highway narrowed. The water finally came into view. It was slick and metallic under the sun. Gorgeous.

"You're welcome," they spoke in unison and for a moment, there was quiet save for the random music.

As we continued easing our way south, I spoke my thoughts aloud. "I forgot how blue it gets down here. It doesn't even look real."

"Neither do your lashes, but here we are," Almaz grinned.

"Ah!" I slapped my knee in shock. "Almaz!" I laughed so hard my stomach tensed. I couldn't believe she said it with a straight face—but I also couldn't stop giggling.

My phone buzzed in the side pocket. I swiped it open, still smiling, expecting Ezra. But it wasn't him. Instead, it was Alex: *Just checking in. Hope the drive is smooth. Let me know if you need anything.*

I stared at the message for a moment. It instantly brought my mood down and made the van feel smaller. I didn't want complexity right now. I wanted ease. How could he think he could just hopscotch back into my life as his schedule allowed?

"You okay, Makeda?" Seble caught my energy shift.

"Fine," I lied. "It's nothing."

Another buzz. This time from Ezra: *Send me a photo of the view. And one of you in it.* Before I could put the phone down, Yemi leaned forward like she smelled a secret.

"Oho! That better not be a man texting for selfies before noon."

That made me yo-yo back into a hearty chuckle.

Almaz twisted around in her seat. "View of what, the water? Or her thighs?"

Seble raised an eyebrow but kept her eyes on the road. "If he starts using words like radiant or divine, we're pulling over for a prayer circle."

Just then, the GPS said, *"Make a U-turn in five hundred feet."*

Seble growled. "God. This thing's possessed."

"Let me do it," Almaz said, reaching for the phone. "You've got us detouring into a swamp."

"Eh, eh! You are *not* touching my screen with greasy cashew hands!"

"Say cashew one more time."

"CASHEW!"

"How about almond to switch it up?"

Yemi threw her hands up. "If we die on this trip, someone better write it down well. I want it to win an award."

"I nominate Makeda, since she's the comeback author among us!" Seble announced. She reached over and squeezed my knee before giving me a wink.

I gave a light smile before leaning my head against the window. The glass was warm against my temple. The Seven Mile Bridge stretched ahead like ribbon pulled taut across the ocean. And for a moment, the noise faded just enough for me to feel the road under us and let the wind thread through my thoughts. Some things deserve my attention now. Some don't. Alex will get a response when it doesn't cost me peace. Doesn't encroach on my joy.

14

SALTWATER & SECRETS

SAME DAY, KEY WEST, FL – LATE AFTERNOON

T he air smelled of salt and grilled fish when we parked, and reggae sneaked out from the back. A sharp citrus scent snaked its way through the soupy atmosphere. Seble eased the SUV into the driveway of the guesthouse, a coral-toned villa with teal shutters and dozens of potted plants. The words *Casa Paloma* were hand-painted in cursive on wood. I already liked it.

A man with silver dreads tucked into a faded *Cuba Libre* baseball cap met us at the gate. "Welcome, ladies," he spoke with an easy grin. "Please...come inside before the sun melts you." A flag tattoo glistened with sweat on his forearm.

"Eh, eh! I thought *we were* the sunshine," Almaz teased. She stepped out in her oversized hat like she was arriving late to Carnival and wanted everyone to notice.

He chuckled and wiped his forehead with a hand towel. "That, too. I just bring the shade." A bead of sweat rolled down his bronzed neck.

Yemi grabbed the first suitcase. "Is it too early to ask for cocktails?"

"Of course not, and please don't trouble yourself with the luggage. I will bring it all inside. Your only task now is to relax," he told her. "My name is Arnoldo, and I will be on hand to help with anything you need."

"Thank you." We spoke in unison with smiles.

Arnoldo gestured for us to proceed with checking in. The slap of his flip-flops against the concrete told us it was definitely time to loosen up.

Inside was a tiled courtyard that wrapped around a cozy pool. Hanging orchids dangled like earrings over wicker chairs. For a split second, they, too, reminded me of Kai, and I smiled. *Maybe I'll shoot some video notes for her.* The kid was always hunting for images of me and the others in her film project. The fact that I'd learned what B-roll was and considered shooting it told me she had more impact on me than I'd given her credit for. I then thought of my finished essay waiting to be read later in our trip. All of this made me feel accomplished and eager to move on to the next steps of sharing my story more broadly while I still had time.

"Seble, great job on choosing this place," Almaz complimented as we got settled.

We had the whole back half of the property—four bedrooms, two baths, a big kitchen we wouldn't touch, and a patio strung with lights. It felt like someone had intentionally prepared it just for women like us. I didn't want to admit how much I *needed* this.

Seble walked straight to the fridge and opened it. "Stocked."

Almaz checked the Wi-Fi. "Decent."

Yemi opened the balcony doors. "God's gift of ocean breeze. Ladies, we will more than survive!"

Unpacking took less than an hour. We showered, changed, and emerged in linen and cotton. Before joining my friends, I glanced in the mirror to see a woman with perfect makeup but a slackness around the eyes I wasn't used to. My face was changing in subtle ways that made it look like a part of me had stepped away and left the rest to pretend. I smiled, forcing my muscles to work, but it still looked like a mask looking back at me. I sighed. This was the new me. I accepted it and moved on before it could unravel the evening.

Traces of lavender, shea, and the faint bite of vetiver oil filled the air we'd all walked through. Dinner was on the patio, and we were blessed with a handsome bartender alongside a Haitian chef named Noelle. She brought out grilled snapper with steam still rising off the top, roasted plantains that caused my mouth to instantly water, and avocado salad. Garlic and thyme rice came out seconds later, rich and fragrant.

"This is heaven," I exclaimed.

"This is how I want to be fed every birthday." Yemi lifted a forkful like she was holding a diamond.

"Skip the birthday. I want this for surviving Monday," Almaz added, already licking her fingers.

There is no greater sign of a perfect meal than a quieted table. Save for a few grunts and pleasurable moans, our group had eventually shut up long enough to enjoy the kind of food you don't talk over. But it lasted only as long as our plates became more filled with bones than the prepared fish.

Almaz broke it. "Yemi, whatever happened with that pastor you were dating? The one with the voice like late-night radio."

"Ugh. He tried to convince me that God had revealed we were meant to marry. Then I found out he was saying the same thing to three other women in the church—one of them a widow!"

The whole table howled.

"Lord, have mercy!"

Even the chef smirked when she swept through to check on the servings.

"Men," Seble soon huffed. "If I was 15 years younger, I'd try women just to see what peace feels like."

"He heeee," Almaz cackled. "You might not be too old to try to catch some fish!"

At this point, admittedly, I nearly lost it. Yemi was doubled over, already gasping for breath. Although Seble was a little quieter than usual. Wine was refilled. Plates cleared. Someone started playing soft music from their phone and Bluetooth speaker. But instead of winding down, the energy turned playful again. I noticed the sky had gone fully dark and mosquitos let us know it was time to spray on the OFF or go to our rooms. We did the former, and we did *not* slow down for long.

The beat caught Almaz's shoulders. Almaz stood first. "Who remembers how to *eskista*?" A dusty krar-string riff tightly looped over drums pumped into the air from the speaker. Her shoulders went first. They were sharp and deliberate, like she'd been waiting for the cue all day. Soon, her eyes closed and the gold hoops in her ears swayed with each movement.

Yemi gave it a go, but her rhythm betrayed her. She burst out laughing, hands on her knees. "Don't tell me I can't remember what used to be my favorite move!"

"That's not it!" Almaz cried. "You're supposed to shake, not snap!"

Kicking off my sandals, I joined in next. Moving with the rhythm. Losing myself in the moment. I moved as if my body hadn't spent most days battling stiffness and aches. I opened myself up to the rhythm of my ancestors and felt not a trace of dis-ease while dancing. There was nothing in my joints, my mind, or my memory holding me back. Only joy. Lost in it, I remembered my mother's arms once stretched like wings. She'd called us into a circle, and we danced until our legs gave out. Even then, we clapped.

But as women in the third quarter of our lives, we danced like there was no one left to impress and only our true selves to remember. We didn't need a crowd or even want shoes. Just a sliver of music and each other. Yemi switched to a version that leaned into Tigrigna—more sway, more weight. Almaz clapped on beat. And I ululated so loud a gecko scampered off the wall.

"Lihihihiii!"

We bopped and laughed and chatted until our sides hurt. From homeland tales to grandkids and lovers just miles away. Gossip. Our heyday. You name it, we talked about it. Between the wine and the food and the conversations, we filled our bellies and our souls with unadulterated sisterhood.

Exhausted, we took everything down several notches and fell out on couches inside. It was late, so we turned off the music, but left a TV on mute in the background. The liquor bottles and glasses were all empty as two of us began dozing off while the others stared into space.

Then in the middle of the quiet we heard a sniffle. It was Seble. Quiet and nearly in the dark, she said, "You know, girls...My husband didn't come home for four days last month."

"What?" I had not seen that coming!

Silence.

"He said he was helping his brother with some property issues in Addis. But every time I called, it went straight to voicemail. No texts or even a *selam*. Just...nothing."

"What did you do?" I quizzed. This was hotter than the scotch bonnet pepper the chef snuck onto the fish!

"I didn't hound his brother or do anything to make a fool of myself. I just sat in it. Like waiting for scraps. Because...I knew." She looked up. "At first, I changed the locks. Then changed them back the day before he returned. I don't know if that makes me wise or weak. Am I not the *wife*?"

No one answered right away. We let the wind do the talking. It rustled the palms. And somewhere nearby, a frog croaked.

Yemi reached across the table and squeezed Seble's wrist.

Almaz said, "It makes you human. Which is more than I can say for half the men I've met."

I didn't offer a story. I really couldn't. Not yet. Instead, I raised my glass. "To still being here."

"To here not being behind us," Seble added.

A beat.

"To love, life, and the lessons we all manage to learn, repeat, and survive."

"Hear, hear," Seble managed a weak smile.

We clinked, drank, and let the cooling night air remind us that change was always coming and all we could do was our best. That night, Almaz took something for sleep. "Only half," she insisted. "Just enough to allow me to have full energy for tomorrow!"

She wandered into the kitchen an hour later, opened the microwave, the dishwasher, the fridge—and walked from one to the next for a long time. "Why did I come in here again?"

We all just shook our heads and rubbed our temples.

Nobody thought much of it—until the wig went missing.

Next Morning, Key West – Midday

I BARELY REMEMBERED FALLING ASLEEP, but I woke to sunlight curling at the corners of the curtain. My body ached in that good way—well-fed, well-laughed, well-loved.

I'd meant to message Ezra the night before, but the wine took hold. I promised myself to do better this morning. Before I joined the others, I snapped a photo of the breakfast spread—papaya, mango, two kinds of toast, butter so soft it practically waved—and another of the patio.

"Look at this. I might never come home!" I texted him. An unruly tremor in my hand reminded me of all the things that

were still waiting for me at home. That followed me here. But I ignored it. Overall, my medication had been keeping them at bay.

He responded minutes later: *"Then I'll come there. And bring better coffee."*

I grinned. Not bad for a man who I still needed to properly communicate with.

The girls and I soon loaded into the van with straw bags, SPF 50, and the buzz of post-breakfast giddiness. Seble had booked a morning snorkeling tour on a reef just off the coast. Our guide, a soft-spoken woman named Camila, handed out fins and masks while warning us that the waves might be "a little chatty today."

"Eh! Eh!" Yemi immediately clutched her stomach.

"Already?" I asked.

"I don't do 'chatty' water," Yemi muttered. "Give me one ginger pill and a prayer, please, girls."

On the other hand, Almaz stepped onto the boat like she was hosting a press conference—new wig and all, although she grumbled about not finding the one she'd worn down. Her swimsuit cover-up was a floor-length floral chiffon cinched at the waist like a sundress. She insisted we capture "a few" photos of her—meaning at least fifteen to capture every angle.

"I'm leaving this entire camera roll to my nieces when I die," she said, flicking her sunglasses down. "Proof that their auntie lived *well*, okay?"

The rest of us just laughed and applied sunscreen before putting on our snorkel gear. The water was pleasantly cool. I eased my way in, letting my limbs go loose. Without even thinking about it, I remembered Ezra's hands on my waist that evening at Dania Beach and the reverie made me blush. Seble squealed from behind her snorkel, snatching me out of the moment, and a school of bright blue fish darted past her like confetti.

"Wow! Look at that!" she pointed out.

We bobbed along together with salt in our mouths and the sun slicking our shoulders. Yemi eventually joined us— though she swore she kept one foot planted on the boat ladder the entire time "just in case God changed His mind."

It was such a liberating, fun, and dynamic time watching the random fish go by and letting myself be free in the ocean again. By the time our tour was over, I was blissfully exhausted.

We had lunch at a long picnic table shaded by coconut-filled palms. I could barely keep my eyes open as the servers brought out platters of grilled shrimp, cracked conch, buttered corn, pineapple slaw, and thick wedges of lime. But I perked up when Almaz pulled a tiny silver flask from her tote.

"I beg your pardon," Seble noticed.

"Oh, it's for the memories, not the buzz!" She motioned at me with her lips. "Pic, pic! Makeda, get this pic with the water in the background for me, no?"

Click. I took it.

Seble smirked. "Suuure."

Almaz then promptly took a sip anyway.

"You know," Yemi started, popping a shrimp into her

mouth, "Seble sharing last night got me to thinking. We should each share something daily."

All of our brows furrowed.

"Something no one else knows, you know? Just for us. Like...how I once helped my ex hide assets from his new wife."

"You *what?*" Almaz nearly choked.

"Oh yeah. He called and said the woman was nosy and greedy. I said, 'Show me the bank statements, and I'll make it all disappear.'"

Seble looked stunned. "But why would you—"

"Because I may not love him anymore, but I wasn't about to let her profit off my past. Besides, I was bored. The process actually taught me a thing or two about spreading assets across countries – not a bad skill to have or thing to do if you can do it."

The table fell silent before breaking into scandalized laughter.

"Remind me *never* to cross you," I quipped.

"Darling," she said, dabbing her lips, "you are not my type."

"Were you not the one talking about it not being too late to catch fish?" I gaggled.

Almaz had no response. Just a tight smile that told me, *you got me!* I wondered if she were really curious about women at this big late age of ours. Truly, it wouldn't matter to me anyway. We all needed to grab peace wherever we might find it.

As we lingered over the last bites, a group of young ladies

at a nearby table kept glancing our way. One finally stood and approached. Her sheer coverall fluttered in the breeze.

"Sorry to interrupt," she smiled shyly. "But y'all are... *everything*. The vibe, the fits, the joy. Just...goals!"

We glanced at one another, caught somewhere between amused and flattered.

"Well, take a good look," Almaz said, waving a plantain chip like a baton. "This is what surviving looks like."

I raised my glass of ginger beer. "And thriving."

The girl grinned. "Yes, ma'am. Do you mind if I take a photo of y'all?"

"Not at all," Almaz answered immediately.

Snap. Snap. Snap. The young woman then headed back to her friends, still grinning. Her presence and compliment made the rest of our afternoon! By the time we headed back for the night, we were spent. And though I still had another full day of activities before I had to read my essay, I still felt a bit of anxiety building about sharing my story. This, on top of persisting thoughts of Alex and how to handle Ezra and the Luther situation made the final hours of my night more exhausting than they should have been.

After showering and bidding goodnight to the girls, I left a quick voice note for Ezra and glanced at my writing before going to bed. I still didn't want to deal with Alex yet. Not during this trip.

I WAS AWAKENED by Almaz's humming off-key through the walls. It was some mix of a church hymn and a Miriam

Makeba chorus. I checked the time. 5:12 a.m. "My God," I grumbled. Were they not the ones teasing me for waking up before the sun? Now on vacation I had been drafted into a sunrise concert I never RSVPed for. As a yawn escaped me, I reached for my phone but put it down after a few moments of not remembering why I'd picked it up. I did that twice before recalling what I was supposed to do: check for an update from my latest scans. The blip passed quickly and there was no new news, but the forgetfulness made me uneasy. Still, I managed to journal for a bit before pressing myself back to sleep for another hour or two. By then, it was time for breakfast.

Footsteps padded in the hallway and the faint clatter of mugs in the kitchen followed. Then the scent of strong coffee crept into the room. My bones ached, but in that full-body, earned kind of way.

Ding. My phone chimed with a handsome *Thinking of you* photo from Ezra.

I pressed the device to my chest with a big grin. Then I did something even more surprising, but not totally foreign to the true me making a return. I captured a photo of my legs stretched out on the bed, sunlight hitting just right. I captioned it: *"Proof of life. Still soft where it counts."* Then I got up and opened the curtains wide. Light filtered through palm leaves and sheer curtains. Another day in Key West.

Fried sweet bread, goat cheese omelets, guava jam, and various teas were laid out for the morning spread. We ate in our robes, laughing about Yemi's refusal to snorkel properly and Almaz's obsession with selfies and capturing the moment rather than being in it. She acted the youngest in the group! But it was cute. Sometimes.

By the time I was back in my room changing for our planned group photo shoot, a ping stopped me mid-button. It was a video from Kai. The frame froze on *me* mid-sentence. Then my voice: *"Some memories punish you for keeping them. Others punish you when you forget."* The clip cut right there. It had no music and didn't fade out. Just the raw words.

Doc B looking fine and dropping bars! Her message read underneath.

I clutched the phone tightly in my hand. My story was coming to life before my eyes in two different mediums. I watched it again in awe of myself on a set even if it was one built by a child. There I was—centered, composed, and almost unafraid. The note from Kai made me more excited to finish my book and share it with anyone who cared to listen.

"Twenty minutes!" Seble sliced through my thoughts.

We were supposed to be changing into our boldest outfits. Color was non-negotiable. Almaz picked a lemon-yellow wrap dress with a dangerous slit. Yemi wore regal emerald linen that made her bronze skin glow. Seble chose a crisp cream jumpsuit. I settled on coral. It was soft and fitted, unapologetically feminine. Each of us had a pair of over-sized sunglasses and white scarves to blow in the wind for the perfect "IG effect" that Almaz wanted. And our hair was pinned up like modern crowns.

Now, the classic car rental was nowhere in our budget, but Seble had insisted, "We did not come this far to take pictures next to a Toyota!" So, we pinched together more funds to lock in a 1957 Chevrolet Bel Air convertible.

It was turquoise and low-slung, clean enough to reflect the waving palms overhead. We parked it on a side street with postcard-worthy sunlight and notable buildings with neon signs in the background. We took turns using the self-timer, testing angles, climbing slightly too far onto the hood until someone's knee cracked loud enough to pause us.

"Alright, but if I end up on a hip replacement list for this shot, somebody better print it big," Yemi groaned.

Our theatrics inevitably caught the attention of a young Black woman walking past with iced coffee, crop top, and bright slides. She slowed down. Her jaw slacked.

"Excuse me," I called out. "Would you mind helping us get a few group shots?"

She looked pleasantly stunned. Really, I was just trying to move this along because we only had an hour left with the car. And I was starting to feel fatigued again.

"Absolutely! Y'all look like rich aunties who survived *everything*."

"He heeee. Right on the mark with that," Seble confirmed.

Soon, several bystanders stopped to photograph us with their phones and the moment became more ridiculous by the second. Random shrieks and finger snaps filled the air.

"Mm hm! Our young photographer encouraged. "Yassssss. Just free, fly, and fine as hell!" Snap. Snap. Pose. Pose.

As she clicked away, I studied her—wide-eyed and moving around us as if we were something rare. And maybe we were.

"Y'all need a soundtrack," someone shouted, and

Afrobeats poured from a random cell phone as we did a few final fun shots. When the first young lady finished, she lowered the phone and said, "Do you mind if I post some? I swear, I'll tag y'all if you want me to. My followers need to see this."

Of course Almaz was the first and only one of us to actually have an Instagram account. "I would love it!"

Then, I stepped toward our young photographer, adjusting my earrings. "Only if you promise me one thing."

She blinked. "Anything."

I smiled. "Make sure you become one of us."

"Yes, ma'am! I am too inspired!"

We let her go. Let the moment go. But it stayed with me.

"One last photo," Almaz pleaded and we obliged.

This time, we held our arms around each other like we'd just stepped out of a glossy magazine spread. Hints of the crowd were barely left by now. We made our way back to the car when my foot clipped the curb. I didn't exactly fall, but I did stagger enough to make the moment stick. Almaz's arm shot out to steady me by the elbow.

"Eh eh, Makeda! We said give them face, not ground," she joked.

"I'm fine," I assured her, catching my breath. "Just got caught up in my own fabulousness."

Yemi smirked. "Better that than one of those damn loose stones. Come. Take it easy, friend. I think we all need some rest now."

We laughed but agreed. Seble also complained of being hot.

Back in the car, I rode in the back with Seble while

Almaz drove. Her spirit dampened but she said nothing, only turning away quickly to peck at her phone. But the screen remained lit up before she could pocket it. A name flashed. Her husband. My gut told me the man had the gall to be checking on her, but I minded my business. It then rang silently again with his name pulsing on the screen. She clicked the side button to send the monitor to black.

"Top down!" Yemi requested. "Let's wrap this up in style, girls!"

It was getting hotter out and the road ahead still waiting.

15

INTAKE

We didn't expect to hear beeping hospital monitors next. We hadn't expected to rush through the whoosh of sliding ER doors to nurses in blue scrubs.

"She was by the pool," Yemi frantically told the clinician. "We'd just come back from a photo shoot and joyride. It was hot. Too hot maybe, and she hadn't eaten much. She stood up too fast, then just—"

"She sat down and then collapsed," I added. "Could it be dehydration or exhaustion? Or...?"

Almaz was near tears. "She said she was overheating, and we didn't take her seriously enough because she said it so easily. Damn it!"

Seble didn't speak as she lay on the white paper. Her lips were chapped and dry. Her eyes stayed on the ceiling.

"Everything is going to be fine," the nurse assured us. "She's stable. Just low fluids and maybe a touch of heatstroke.

We're running tests, but she should be okay to leave in a few hours," she comforted us before slipping out.

In that moment, Almaz cracked a joke about needing a margarita drip, but it didn't land. The mood was too angst-filled.

Yemi reached for Seble's hand. "You scared us."

"Do you want us to call Moses?" I asked softly.

Seble blinked once. Then, quiet but clear: "No, not yet. If this isn't serious, then I don't want him rushing down here during the little bit of time we have left. I will be fine."

That was all.

Within two hours, she was walking steadily and easily following basic instructions. Her tests came back clean—no underlying cardiac or neurological issues, so we were cleared to go.

"Just make sure you stay hydrated," the nurse told us. "And no strenuous activity for the next 24 hours. Take it easy."

Almaz glanced at the clipboard at the front desk upon checkout. "Please tell me we won't have to max out a credit card for this," she whispered.

Seble signed everything and took the forms. "Not at all. I'll handle it." She slipped it into her tote.

No one asked how. It was none of our business.

WE TOOK it easy for the rest of the day. Back at the pool, yes, but with all the umbrellas drawn and a steady flow of cool water and iced tea. The chef brought out cold melon soup and chicken salad sandwiches. At some points we dozed off. Others, we nattered in low tones while watching the clouds change shape.

The mood had shifted. None of us were performing. Not for the camera. Not for each other. And as the clock ticked on, Almaz eventually reminded us that she never got to share her secret.

"Might as well spill it now," I encouraged, knowing I hadn't shared one either.

She took the downtime to confess that she was briefly engaged to a gay man decades ago.

"He was a great guy. But that was something neither of us could change about him, so I helped him come out but never told anyone until now," she spoke with a soft exhale. "I wore the ring for six months. Still have it." She touched her ring finger.

It was quiet for a while after that. We let the moment breathe, knowing that not every truth needed commentary— just a place to land. The lack of voice and song and everything else felt just as good as the ruckus we'd been causing all along. We sank into it.

Later that night, we retreated to the porch and enjoyed the cushioned rocking chairs. Everything felt easy again. There was no music and no wine; however, we'd had enough. Seble had a tall glass of cool water and Almaz encouraged us to drink ginger tea. The air still held warmth, but the sky gave up its color. This is when I unfolded the first page of my first paper and cleared my throat before I let myself think too hard.

"You guys still up for hearing my writings?"

A collective gasp at me having the nerve to ask.

"Woman! We've waited all weekend for this."

"You better start reading!"

I smiled nervously and cleared my throat before beginning... "Alright. It's called 'Silence is a Heavy Inheritance.'"

Immediately, there were head nods and soft murmurs.

I held my head up and began... "I was raised on voices. Voices rising and falling. Laughter spilling freely as tej at family weddings. The voices were just as loud as the colors streaking through concrete. Our home in Addis overflowed with sounds—the scrape of chairs being pulled close and gossip passing fervently. Except for the spaces in between... brief pauses where something almost got said but didn't, or moments when elders' eyes met across the room to choose carefully what truths a child could bear. Those silences weren't cruel, but they were cautious. Protective, even. Until one day caution became habit, and that habit became inheritance," I glanced up, "and suddenly, I was carrying silences I never intended.

Losing my voice with age wasn't the hardest part. It was realizing how long I'd been quiet to keep the peace."

I took a beat to veer from my essay. "Tonight, in front of you, my dearest friends, I am achieving the first step of many to completely reclaim my voice."

"Hear, hear!" Seble spoke first.

"On the page, in my life, and before my body forgets how," I finished.

The only sound in the room now was the soft click and whir of a ceiling fan above.

Almaz wiped the corner of her eye with the back of her

hand, then scoffed at herself. "Now why did you go and do that to my mascara?" She stood up and walked around my chair, wrapping her arms around me from behind. She rested her chin on my shoulder. "I am damn proud of you, sister. This is going to be phenomenal. I know it."

"Honestly, it is great motivation for all of us to be more vocal before we are erased, no?" Yemi added.

"Thank you," I smiled, and we shared a brief and beautiful moment of sisterhood before they goaded me to finish the rest.

The remaining essay passages were about the difference between quitting and protecting yourself. About generational absence and the false security of secrets. It was about learning to build a new language with the breath you still have—one that doesn't ask permission to name what hurt.

I set the pages down while my heart punched out a bassline in my chest. We were quiet again for a while before Seble cut through it.

"If you finish that book," she announced, "I'll find a way to get it into print. I don't care if we have to sell injera door to door!"

"He heeeee!" Almaz raised her tea like it was the most exquisite champagne. "To no more invisibility."

Yemi tapped her mug to ours. "To no more performing fine."

I beamed. "And no more waiting."

We clinked assuredly.

"Wait!" Almaz shouted before we could drink. "Let's do that again so I can get a little video for social media!"

"Ayyyy, Egziabher!" Yemi groaned. *Oh, God.* But we all did it. That moment felt like promise.

"Makeda, please tell me that man of yours knows you're leaving all this behind tomorrow." Seble quizzed me while we began gathering our things for the final day.

"Yes, if you must know."

But it was when Almaz paused in the hallway like she'd seen a ghost that stopped us all mid-step.

"Okay, girls, seriously," she began. "I am missing something really important."

"Your phone?" Yemi guessed.

"Driver's license?" I tried.

"No! My damn Sunday wig!" Almaz snapped.

"Didn't you pack that already?"

"I packed my *everyday* wig. My *don't-talk-to-me-on-a-Tuesday* wig. I have my *high-holy, curl-defining, edges-laid-down-by-the-Lord* wig. But I still can't find my *Sunday* wig!" she cried.

A search began. Under beds. In drawers. Near the pool. In the dryer. We even looked between couch cushions, like it might have wandered off on its own.

Then Almaz gasped. "Wait."

She jogged into the kitchen and opened the microwave. Nothing. The dishwasher. Still, nothing. "Oh, come on!" Then... she opened the freezer."

A burst of cold air hissed into the room.

A collective gasp with hands on chests. There it was! Sitting proudly on top of the key lime pie.

"What in the world?!" Yemi muttered.

The ice maker clattered loudly, like it couldn't take the tension either.

"Oh my god," I whispered, clutching the counter. "Almaz."

She lifted it gently, unfazed. "That Ambien is a menace. Ugh!" The same pill she took to help her sleep apparently helped her sleepwalk.

"Should we...be worried?" I asked between wheezes.

"Only if she puts it back in," Yemi deadpanned.

"No!" Almaz sniffed the synthetic hair. "Still smells fresh though. Minty even."

"That is not mint. It's frostbite!"

We lost it. One of us slid to the floor. Another tried to take a photo and dropped the phone. Eventually, the wig was placed on the countertop like a crowned roast.

Almaz posed next to it, fist under chin. "Tag it: Icon. Legend. Wigcicle."

And that's how we ended the night: Cry-laughing and holding our bellies. None of us were sure if we were losing our minds or just finally free enough to enjoy them.

It didn't matter. Someone opened a bag of chips and we committed to finishing the final bottle of wine. We were deliciously busy being alive.

16

NOISE IN THE QUIET

MAE'S APARTMENT, COCONUT GROVE, FL

I kicked off my shoes by the door the moment I got back to my apartment. *My, my, my.* I was worn out in the best way. There was so much to unpack, from my clothes and notes to the ridiculous collection of new memories we managed to make in just a few days. And to the honesty we all shared. My heart was full, and my mind was primed for next steps.

I dragged my suitcase into my room and plopped down on the bed for a breather. The apartment needed air, but I was too tired to get up again and open windows, so I just lay there for a spell.

Be-beep! My cell phone chirped beside me. "Doc B!" It was a voice note from Kai. "I hope you enjoyed your trip. I have more video clips to share with you—almost done with all the edits, you know? This is going to be a dope project! Let me know when you can meet up at the Center. I know you've been out there living your best life so rest up then hit me up," she added.

I liked that kid more and more as time went on. She was so energizing, a contrast to myself in the moment. "Get up, Makeda," I goaded myself after listening. *Absolutely not,* another part of me countered. *Rest if you want to. Everything will still be there when you* want *to get up.* The dual me's were an unexpected return to a struggle I always had when younger: push through or pull back. But today, I needed to go with discipline. I didn't have time for too much leisure, especially after just enjoying it for days on end with my friends. The clock was ticking, and I had a book to write, a man to call, and a son to sort out.

I got up and opened my balcony doors then put things in their proper place before brewing a pot of coffee. I texted Kai back to let her know I was in the zone and had just seven more essays to write to complete my book. *I'm ready to learn more about self-publishing*, I told her. *I want to know what the best options are.*

The next day Ezra and I met at the Coconut Grove Farmers market. We'd missed each other and didn't want to pretend we didn't. Late morning found us walking through a shaded path between fruit stalls. It was a Tuesday, so the crowd was thin but still speckled with life.

English, Spanish and Creole chatter rose from behind tables while I clutched a small basket with plantains and ginger. I was still missing my favorite ground coffee from a local roaster.

"It looks like you ladies had a hell of a vacation," Ezra

commented on my girls' trip. Sunlight filtered through the banyan trees overhead as we strolled.

"We did," I smiled. "Too much food, too much sun, so many truths. The good kind, though.... the kind that might sting a little before settling in."

"Sounds like therapy with better outfits."

"I guess you could call it that."

The sounds of a steel drummer playing an almost melancholic rhythm wafted through the air. *South Florida*...such a fusion of Black culture. I loved it. Ezra and I continued walking with our sorrel iced teas, passing rows of produce and handmade soaps before he signaled that he wanted to sit down for a bit.

"No samples unless you buying, baby!" a vendor barked at someone dipping their fingers into a mango spread.

That's nasty work, as Kai would say, the phrase popped into my mind as a chuckle left my lips.

"Careful, now. Folks are crazy." Ezra nudged me to a bench under a tamarind tree with a hand on the small of my back.

For a few minutes, we just sat there people-watching as the fruit tree cast a dappled net of shadows over our wooden seat. Ezra took another sip from his tea. I stopped drinking mine. Debating. Then acting.

"I've been meaning to ask you something, Ez," I spoke up. "And honestly, it's not because I need a dramatic reveal. I just don't want to keep avoiding it because it's been bothering me."

He looked over. Neutral. "Alright."

"Well, we never discussed what's going on with you and

your brother. And… after the way he spoke to you at the poetry event—what he said to me—it's not something I can file under the 'before we met' category."

Ezra exhaled slowly through his mouth, nostrils flaring.

"He said you burned the last bridge you had," I continued. "That you disappear when it counts."

"Ah, Mae! He's been rehearsing that one a long time!"

"Well, I don't know if that's fair, but I need to understand what kind of fracture is between you two, and the rest of your family, if any."

Ezra flexed his jaw, struggling to not look at me.

"I want to know if I'm standing next to someone who walks away then pretends nothing is lost. That's all," I pressed.

A beat.

"Ezra?"

"Okay, Mae. It's like I told you before. We started something together. A business. I walked away from it, and from him. And he's still mad. That's the short version."

I knew a half-truth when I heard one. But I also knew to slow down enough to choose my next words carefully when the person who gave it mattered. Ezra sat back. His fingers tightened around the paper cup. He huffed. "Luther sees it as abandonment. I see it as boundaries. Not every fight needs a second round, you know?"

"I understand, and I agree. But. What. Actually. Happened?"

Ezra rubbed his palms against his thighs. Once. Then again. "There was a job," he relented. "A private security system installation tied to a city developer Luther hated. The man had a reputation for buying up family land under the table. Luther said no. That we don't touch blood money. He said it was about dignity."

His voice was low and controlled, but I heard the old rust in it. "I took it anyway. It was good money!" Ezra paused and I let it hang in the air. I didn't want to fill in any space for him that allowed escape. "But that wasn't the real break," Ezra continued. He sniffled and scratched his widow's peak. "Our mother was also sick that year. She was slipping faster than I ever realized because I had been away. Said I was busy. Said I'd come home when I wrapped the big project."

My eyes widened. Waiting.

"I didn't make it in time." Ezra looked down. His words sank like a body no one came looking for.

I didn't move.

"Luther was there every day. He cleaned her, talked to her even when she didn't know who he was, and...he held all that grief on his own while I just sent money."

My stomach tightened.

"He didn't freeze me out right away," Ezra kept going. "I showed up after she passed and helped with the arrangements. I carried the casket, hosted the gatherings and said the right things in the midst of my own burden of guilt for being an unforgivable son."

Ouch. His last two words sliced me clean open. I felt my own lips tighten and quiver. *Alex?* Could he ever think that about himself? Was he? Is Ezra what Alex might be in twenty years if we never reconcile? Was that even my problem since he's the one who left? What might my end look like if I did nothing else?

Ezra let out a sharp breath that brought me back to him and the moment.

"But everything from the funeral prep to the service and burial, to the family gathering afterwards was all through gritted teeth. Mostly Luther's. We didn't speak more than necessary. I didn't know how. I felt *everything*, but not a word about it made it to my mouth. So...I just moved through it like men do when everything underneath is cracked. I locked my feelings up in an old box inside myself and moved on."

"Mmph." His pain was contagious, but I bucked against it. "So, you guys just stopped talking after that?" I touched his knee. It was too hard to not comfort at all.

"Not right away, no," he explained. "It wasn't until that city developer job came up. That's when it all came out. Not just the install. Everything."

"What did he say?"

"He said I only show up when someone needs a hero. And when real presence is required...I vanish."

"Is that true?"

"No!"

A beat.

"But I didn't fight back. I just packed my tools and left the business. I let him keep the name and the anger. I thought it was cleaner that way. I didn't want to feel anything anymore."

"But now?" My mind was spinning.

Ezra shrugged. "Now I live with it. And so does he." We both stopped to let out a breath before Ezra spoke again. "But eventually...I did want to feel again. Something. Anything. So, I fought for that. You're meeting a much better version of me, Mae. But I'm no saint. I still have to live with my bad decisions. I'll have to die with them."

I nodded, but something in me recoiled. I had nothing in me to comfort him regarding this and knew that wasn't my job anyway. The moment between us got louder without another word from him or me. Soon, I stood up to stretch my legs before tossing my cup into the nearest trash bin. Ezra didn't get up from the bench.

I turned to face him. "What was she like?"

"Who?"

"Your mother."

His gaze shot back down. "Sharp as vinegar, but often much quieter than she had to be."

"Sounds familiar."

That got half a smile. Then silence again—but this time, it didn't press on us.

"There's nothing for me to win with Luther," he got up and extended his limbs.

"Oh, I wasn't asking you to win, Ezra. I just wanted to understand what part of that tension you take ownership of for yourself. Thank you for telling me."

"Mm hm." We started walking again. "I can do more work on me," he grumbled, and we left it at that.

THE DAYS that followed blurred into small routines—a bookstore run for a new title, grocery shopping, more hand-writing and voice notes transcribed. I made exactly the amount of progress on my book that I expected, because once I *expected* to, my actions ensured it. Five essays spilled into six, then seven. My goal was to publish it in the next thirty days.

Seble dropped off a meal here and there—even starting a marketing plan for me. Almaz reminded me of exercise we should be doing together, and Yemi sent an article on memory loss with a voice note that said, "We're doing the hard things now." Ezra sent me photos of a banyan tree with no caption. And I reached out to Kai to schedule our next session. I wanted to view more of the footage she'd shot. Momentum took root although I hadn't spoken to Alex yet. That bent piece of the puzzle still didn't fit neatly in my life.

I left my apartment to visit a neighborhood café filled with chatter, music, and waiters who dodged each other's trays with ease. With a half-eaten peach pastry by my elbow, I kept writing.

I scrawled notes on a napkin when my notebook ran out of pages. Somewhere between a baby wailing behind me and a man trying to impress his date in three languages, the world present faded out. A part of me kept reaching back in time to find the right words for my essay, "The Sound of Landing." *What to say, what to say, what to say?* I kept wondering before closing my eyes and floating back further than my days in young motherhood, further than my marriage itself. My mind drifted back to that first year I arrived in the United States with hands hungry for purpose and a tongue hesitant in every room. The country was an incredibly strange land, and I had never seen so many white people before, kind and indifferent...

Washington, DC — Winter 1980

IT WAS COLD. Frigid. Even in the heated building with my hands and ambition tucked into the sleeves of my borrowed coat, I froze. I had no idea what counted as courage and what counted as survival, but I swallowed the knot in my throat as the woman behind the desk stamped my paperwork like it was any other Tuesday. She made eye contact but offered no smile. Still, I could never forget the dull thud of a rubber seal hitting bureaucracy.

"Congratulations," she handed me my documents. "You've been granted asylum. Welcome to the United States, Ms....Ma...keeeda...Bee--kele?" She tried her best with my name.

That was it. There was no music or star-spangled banner. Only fluorescent lights and a laminated poster about tuberculosis screening—and a photo of President Ronald Reagan next to an American flag. I stepped outside into the winter air and stared up at the falling snow. White. Slow. Cool. Magical. It was beautifully strange. I felt it crunch underfoot, and the whole moment was surreal to me. With my eyes closed and my feet grounded, I welcomed the second chance at life I'd gotten. Sure, it meant I had to reimagine my entire life and learn new ways and customs, but I was alive. I'd made it!

At just 20 years old, I stood still for a long moment, letting the frost settle into my lungs, even took my hands out of my pockets to feel what the other side of survival was like.

Still so young, I didn't yet know the name for the feelings I had, but I knew they were mine. I just breathed.

Looking around, I noticed how the snow wasn't pretty everywhere—just the untouched patches. The rest had already turned to dirty slush at the curb, darkened by foot-prints and engine grease. And yellowed by dog pee.

"Eh, at least it's honest," I'd mumbled to myself.

When making my way to the church-run shelter that was housing me for the following weeks, the cold of the snow hitting my brown skin unconsciously shifted to visions of dust whipping beneath thatch straws and hole-filled canvas flaps in Nairobi, Kenya. More memories. Deeper into my past now. I recalled the heat of my *first stop* after Ethiopia. It had not been the United States—how I'd wished it was. But instead, it was a Kenyan refugee camp.

The compound was on the outskirts of Nairobi. Stressful. Dangerous. Like living in a daily fire, and every morning I wanted to run away. But I needed healthcare and food and clothes, so I stayed. Remembering how I'd gotten *there*, and it wasn't through weakness or luck. I had decided to live and had chosen exile over silence in my homeland. I'd fled when the revolution became too dangerous for me to speak against it. When it was "shut up or death."

In Nairobi, the air inside the compound was hot. It always smelled like sweat, unwashed bodies, ash, and scorched maize flour. My nose could never forget the rank medley. Tin bowls scraped loudly at dawn and my back had ached from the cheap cots. But it was the uncertainty that hollowed my stomach most.

Still, every time they called names from the clipboard, I

stood straighter. Hoping. And when mine was finally called —I *knew*. The next place would break me in new ways, but it would not break me completely. I would thrive, because I gave myself no choice but to. And then suddenly I was there. In the United States. Shaking off the recollections of the refugee camp, I willed myself back to the present. Back into the white winter wonderland of 1980s Washington, DC.

Focus, I thought. *This is your new home now*. I pushed open the brown church door and stepped into the makeshift shelter's warmth. Soft murmurs, instant coffee, and a table full of pastries greeted me.

"Welcome!"

"Welcome."

"Hello there, young lady."

Friendly greetings and religious smiles were everywhere. I distrusted the latter but was grateful for it all the same. An unfamiliar detergent met me when I was escorted to my tiny room. My new life already sounded so much different. Less stressful. Less dangerous. And more like a heat that could help or hurt you, but at least there was an option between the two. I had a *real* mattress.

Praise Allah—or..."Thank God!" As the Americans said. The smile of a conqueror rose on my face. Indeed, I had survived what was meant to end me and still had the nerve to imagine a future. Little did I know how many more chapters of my life would break me open and challenge me to continuously be better. That there is never a resolute "I made it" in life.

17

RED PEN, CLEAN HANDS
PRESENT DAY, MIAMI, FL

P rogress. I printed all eleven essays and laid them on the dining table like bones on an altar. Warm daylight rays hit my skin through my sliding glass door and the distant sound of my neighbor's wind chimes pulled their own song out of the breeze. Incense burned on a shelf behind me.

I had finished the first full draft of my book. My heart thudded as I looked over my words. My life. My truths. Recalling pieces from memory here and there was one thing, but capturing key events over six decades was another completely. I'd been so many women during this time. I had felt so much. Seen so much. Loved so much. Lost so much. I couldn't believe how fast I'd gotten the manuscript done. The process itself also taught me how much I'd discovered how to *be* and *move* throughout my life. Mistakes were made, but I'd learned so much.

The more I looked at the essays in the quiet of my apartment, the more I realized I wanted more than just my friends, Kai, and a few random people on the internet to read it. I wanted it to be *felt* by anyone it could help—younger women who don't yet have the words for what they've survived. Who think starting over disqualifies them from being whole. Or who have been told too many times that grief should have an expiration date. Life was too long and complex for that.

The words in those pages were loaded but needed a professional eye to strip the indulgent and sharpen what could pierce hearts—that much I knew to be true. It wasn't even ready for Seble, Yemi, or Almaz. Not yet. They would ask questions too early or see all of me in the manuscript and try not to flinch. I needed an editor who didn't care about my feelings in the deep way my friends did. That's when I remembered Candace R. King.

I'd met her years ago on a panel in D.C. Retired from a major press, her voice and encouragement stayed with me longer than her bio did. In that moment, I pulled out my laptop and opened the email I never deleted, hoping she still used it. "If you ever write a book," she'd said, "I want to read it."

I hit "reply."

Minutes later, my shoulders deflated when the message came back undeliverable, but I was determined to find her. I searched social media—everything from Facebook to LinkedIn—until I found her. With such a common first name, it took diligence and digging, but I knew in my heart she was the one. And indeed, she remembered me.

Candace responded with more enthusiasm than I expected. "Dr. Makeda Bekele!" she wrote. "You have no idea how often I've wondered about you and if you ever told your story! I meant what I said back then." Candace was still selectively editing projects in retirement, but said she'd be honored to work with me. She asked for a sample to start. "Send me the one that took the longest to write."

And with that, my goal became even more real. It wasn't like I hadn't published books before, but they were all non-fiction, academic, and tied to a university press. This was the blood, flesh, and breath of my life and I wanted it to be healthy. I didn't want it changed too much to be "marketable" to masses either, I realized, so I also wanted to keep control. I was hopeful to bring its quality to the next phase with Candace's help and then figure out the printing and distributing on my own in the next few weeks. I didn't want to waste years trying to shop it around in hopes that some agent and traditional publisher would pick me. I might not have many good years left.

THE NEXT MORNING, Alex called. I didn't answer. Instead, I decided to put down my pen and pick up my phone. *His father should know about his resurrection*, I thought. It was the least I could do after I'd laid on him—Robert—how Alex's absence made me feel like a worthless mother.

I kept the call short but intentional. Told him our son had reached out, and that I actually saw him and his *big* moment at a local restaurant. Robert was flummoxed, asking when, how, what I made of it. I answered what I could and left the rest alone. He was quiet for a while before saying, "I'm really glad to hear that. He's still yours even if he doesn't know how to be. And we're all still family, even if decisions scattered us more than we meant it to. Thanks for letting me know, Mae."

"Of course," I expelled a relieved breath. I wasn't sure what I was calmed about, but Robert's words made my shoulders relax. I was grateful for that.

After we hung up, I stayed slouched in my chair. My eyes drifted across the room until they landed on the lower shelf of my bookcase. A small, dusty frame was half-tucked behind a candle. A child's image stared back at me. Alex... at maybe six or seven. I squinted and got up to get a closer look. Picking up the photo, I saw that we were at a street fair, and he was grinning with a half-eaten pretzel in one hand and a juice box in the other. A mustard stain was on the corner of his Batman shirt, and the photo was crooked in its frame.

"My, my..." I whispered, while opening the back to straighten it. An uncertain slight smile tugged at my lips.

The image was taken in D.C. Summertime. And the brown-skinned, blue-eyed boy was having the time of his life with Robert and me. He'd pestered me incessantly about getting his name on something—his own cup, his own towel, a little wooden sign for his bedroom door.

"Please, mommy, please!" I could still hear his squeaky little voice in all its cuteness as he begged for something official. Something that said *this is **mine**. And he wanted his whole name: Alex Jeffrey Jones.*

I blinked. The middle name. He'd named his hotel after it. It was his father's, too. *Nothing of me...* The omission realization made me spring up with a wild thought. Pacing didn't help. Tea didn't help. I didn't feel like writing. And I didn't feel like sitting still. I grabbed my keys and headed out. Fifteen minutes later, I pulled into a metered space across from The Jeffrey Hotel.

The building rose confidently—a Mediterranean revival of carved stone and wrought iron balconies. Warm yellow light spilled through tall windows, making the lobby chandelier shimmer even from across the street. At first, I stayed in my car, watching a slender doorman dressed in all black save for a red cap and pocket square. He looked familiar, but I couldn't place him. He also looked like an easy-going guy who had seen every kind of entrance: confident, desperate, drunk, joyous, broken. He nodded when he caught me looking and offered a smile before slipping off with someone's luggage.

I got out. Against what I'd told myself to do, I felt my feet striding past two metal signs marked Owner and Reserved Parking—with no one parked in either space—to the front doors and the *whoosh* of them automatically opening. Cool air and fancy air freshener greeted me instantly. Something in my chest bloomed, either pride or panic. Why was I here? What did I expect? I had no idea.

I walked in like I had business there, which I did, just not in a way anyone would expect. But I didn't want to bring attention to myself, so I quickly moved about the lobby and down a short hallway where a sign said there would be restrooms. A petite, sharp-eyed woman whose name tag read: "Ana," passed me in the hallway, arm full of linens. She smiled warmly and nodded enthusiastically. Nothing clicked in her expression. I was no one. Just another old woman with good posture and a bag slung across her chest. She moved on.

I walked the loop once, taking in how nice the hotel was. I knew Alex wasn't there because the owner's space out front was empty—but that wasn't why I came. Something in me needed to know if his life turned out as perfect as he wanted it to be without me... if building a legacy without ever glancing over his shoulder had been as easy as dusting off his past. From the looks of it, it was. That made my heart sink.

Just then, a cheerful Latino man greeted me.

"How can I help you, ma'am?" His name tag read Marco.

"Oh...nothing. I thought my son was staying here, but um...I was mistaken. Turns out he's at the Vestige hotel up the street."

"Ah, I see," he grinned. "Well, if he's in town again in the future, I hope he gives The Jeffrey a try."

Quite the salesman, I thought before politely walking out. Back in the car, I let the engine run for a minute before pulling away. I had seen enough. Tomorrow, I'd meet with someone who hadn't lived any of this but would still get to read everything.

18

LINES BETWEEN THE PAGES

"Mae, time did nothing to dull your edge." Candace and I met early the next morning via video chat. "I read your essay twice before I picked up my pen." She looked just as I remembered, only sharper. Close-cropped silver curls. Bronze skin. Earrings that swung like punctuation. If anyone embodied the power of the pen, it was her.

"I'm so glad to reconnect with you," I spoke honestly. "Never actually thought I would write everything down like this."

"How does it feel? I'm thrilled that you reached out!" Candace's eyes were warm. She was framed by the soft edges of plants and a bookshelf that sat in the distance behind her.

"Strange but right."

She chuckled. "Totally understand. Welcome to non-academic writing."

Candace and I hadn't spoken in nearly eight years—not

since that panel at Howard where we sat side by side and dissected memoirs that made people feel seen. I wasn't there as a writer. I'd been invited for context as a professor and forensic linguist with firsthand experience most scholars only study. Back then, I had shared bits and pieces of my life but chose to keep most of it close. Candace caught me afterwards and told me to keep in touch if I ever decided to put it all down because "I could feel that there's so much more to you." And now...I had.

We talked as if not much time had passed. She caught me up on her latest clients and the essays she'd helped turn into conversations bigger than the page. I filled in the outlines of my life in recent years slowed me down. The rest. The gains. The losses. The new possibilities. The tremor in my hands I no longer bothered to hide and the creep of a myriad of other symptoms that came with my new position in life.

Eventually, she held up my sample chapter to pivot to business. "Mae, this essay is sharp. It's clean... truthful without begging for sympathy, and that's rare. I marked a few sections—mostly rhythm work and clarity. There is one part where I think you intentionally stopped digging before it got too deep, but overall...this? If all of your essays are like this, then your collection will be *perfect* to shop around! You could land a serious agent with this!"

I exhaled. That wasn't the path I wanted, but I let her finish. Candace then went through a deeper explanation of what she'd edited and why she'd made certain comments.

"You've got a striking voice, but you did slip into academic distance in a few lines. Pull that back. Let this sound like *you*—not a lecture, because readers will stay for your voice, not your credentials."

I nodded, fully understanding her critique.

"The arc in this essay works really well," she continued. "It speaks to the present moment and memory and insight, but if every piece follows that map, your collection risks feeling predictable. Do you have a piece that's just...bare? No scaffolding or no arc?"

"I have to check."

"One with truth that stings. Readers need a few of those at least. Essays in the voice that says, 'I didn't write this for you. I wrote it because I had to.' That's what will make this collection feel alive versus assembled."

I smiled, appreciating all of her feedback. "Got it."

Candace set the pages down. "I'd love to read it and give more solid notes on the rest, but only if you're ready to be challenged."

"I certainly am."

"Awesome!"

That was it. I hired her. The clock was ticking, and I needed to get this book done while I still could because I could already notice my handwriting getting smaller and unreadable—another unpleasant indication of Parkinson's. Between that and the unexplained exhaustion that recently started hitting me, I knew I was in a race against myself. But I was excited at the prospect of publishing another version my life story! I even thought to add two more essays to the collection that I'd been afraid to breathe new life into. It felt right now. I had nothing to lose by telling it all, especially on the journey of motherhood.

I got to work on them.

MORE THAN A WEEK passed since I'd heard from Alex again. He didn't try to reach me again after I didn't answer his last call. *Damn it.* Maybe I should have picked up whether I was ready to reconcile or not. Either way, I wasn't going to revisit his hotel like a lunatic. I did send him a text message requesting to meet. The ball was in his court again. This time, I would play if he responded. It was time.

With my collection done, including the two new ones, I sent the file to Candace for a full manuscript edit. The next thing was to meet Kai to watch our footage. She was out of school on break and said the entire thing was done.

"I'll be at the Center today if you want to come through, Doc B," she told me in a video note. Her smile was quick and bright, and she had a new style to her braids. I could hear traffic behind her—the afternoon buzz—and knew she was already on the move.

"I'm on my way," I told her.

But en route to my car, I felt unsteady. My balance was off, and I had a gut feeling not to drive myself anywhere. The intuition broke my heart, but I listened. It was too deep not to. Plus, I knew that falling was another problem I'd have to deal with eventually and didn't want to risk a freak early appearance. Yet I was desperate to move forward and meet Kai, so I phoned Yemi for a ride. The request was humbling but a million times better than those senior vans many people my age had to rely on. I was *not* looking forward to ever needing one of those. Nothing wrong with them, I just didn't want to be in one.

I went back to the lobby area to wait for Yemi, who pulled up to the building fifteen minutes later wearing a deep indigo caftan. She gave an empathetic smile and wave as I moved from the curb to her car door.

Once inside, she reached over and rested her palm lightly on my knee. "You alright, Makeda?" Her hair was pulled back into a low twist that allowed the gold studs in her ears to glisten. Even without makeup, Yemi always looked composed.

I nodded. "Just needed a little help today."

Yemi pursed her lips and nodded affirmatively. With two taps to the steering wheel, she said. "Alright. Let's roll."

It didn't take long to get there and she drove with ease. "Text me when you're done," she told me. "I'll be nearby. No rush."

"Thanks, sis." I truly was grateful.

Kai was in a screening room, earbuds looped around her neck while her phone and laptop sat in front of her when I found her.

"Ayyy, Doc B. It's good to see you." She got up for a hug. "It's been a while."

"Love the new scent," I complimented. Her perfume smelled like a mix of mandarin and neroli oil with a sugar finish.

"Appreciate that. Guess it settled into my skin just right."

Kai soon dimmed the lights, and the room darkened to a small theatre. Only the glow from her computer illuminated the space.

She wanted to show me the teaser first before cutting to

my section. The trailer began with grainy, high-contrast pictures. Archival photos of me and the two other interview subjects swiped across the screen like an old newsreel. The transitions were sharp, yet it had minimal motion. Black and white. No soundtrack yet. Just the room tone and the soft mechanical click between cuts. It felt deliberate. The final shot held on my face mid-breath, before cutting to black. A title appeared in plain white text: **"Voices We Almost Lost."** Then came Kai's name, tucked in the corner like a footnote in small font.

It was only 29 seconds, but it stole my breath. "Very nice, Kai. Very nice!" I was genuinely excited to see my segment. A little nervous too.

She beamed. "It's not even done yet. I still have to balance the sound and color-grade your segment. But I wanted you to see the arc." She clicked a few keys, and the screen jumped. My own voice came in mid-sentence, clipped at the start. She adjusted the playback. "This is where I start you," she told me, not looking away from the screen. "I cut in from silence without any music under it, so it's just your clear and bare voice."

My face appeared. I was seated near the altar in my apartment, speaking slowly, unsure of where I was going yet. The light hit just one side of my face. My hands stayed folded in my lap the entire time. It looked...still.

Kai watched me watch myself.

The footage soon got more interesting. More rhythm and emotion. She'd edited in images from my home, archival protest footage she'd found, and old family photos of me that I'd let her scan. It was well edited and sharp. Watching me tell my life story and knowing my book was with a professional editor made me feel alive. Except I had said nothing about having a son during the video interviews. The reality of that hit me hard. While I made sure I wasn't erased, I'd omitted a literal part of me and that didn't feel right, especially since I'd written essays about it.

"What's wrong, Doc?" Kai quizzed me.

"Nothing." I remained lost in thought.

"Was there something you don't like?" She pressed.

"No. Not at all. It looks great."

"So....then...what's up, Doc?"

"There's something missing."

"What?"

"A final truth."

"And that is?"

"My son."

"Your what?"

I'd never told her I had a child. "We have a complicated relationship."

"I see." Kai stayed quiet for a beat. Then she scratched the back of her head, a nervous habit I'd seen before. "I mean...you don't *have* to put that in the doc," she spoke carefully. "But...shouldn't it be there?"

I didn't answer.

Kai shifted her weight and glanced at the paused frame on her screen. "I don't know what it's like to have a kid or fall out with one, but...if it's part of what made you *you*, then leaving it out kinda feels like...editing history? The exact reason we're doing this to go against that, right? To have no shame or skip the parts that actually matter just because they hurt." She looked at me again. "But if it's too much, I get that. It does explain something though. Like, I don't know what exactly, but I *felt* it in your silences."

"I should add it. But not today."

"You've got time."

But I didn't believe that—not anymore. My body had been uttering different terms lately, and I'd wasted enough years telling myself there would always be a later. She got up to turn on the room lights.

"Alright then. Let's include it. Let's get it done."

Kai's grin returned, wide and relieved. She tapped her laptop. "Say the word, Doc B, and I'll bring the camera tomorrow. You're the center of this. It doesn't work without you."

I looked at the screen again. The image was frozen on me mid-sentence, eyes in motion, hands unmoving. "Tomorrow," I confirmed.

She gave a tiny fist pump. "You got it."

And just like that, I felt the hourglass tip.

Kai also floated the Miami Documentary Festival deadline a few times—always in passing, like a dream we could maybe share. But that was different. My book had structure, timelines, edits. This film felt like a racehorse out of the gate. Looser. More exposed. One project felt like my voice in my hands. The other felt like I was being carried by someone else without pause. Still, part of me wanted to say yes. To both. To all of it. Now. Before anything else slipped away, but I confirmed nothing. Kai meant well and handled everything so far with care, but my arms crossed before I knew I needed the barrier.

19

HALF THE STORY

The next three weeks flew by. Alex did eventually reply to my message with a voice memo saying he unexpectedly had to leave the country but would call again once everything was sorted out. He sounded disheveled, and despite everything between us, that worried me. Even though he didn't say where he was, why, or how long he'd be gone, something in me braced. We still hadn't had a proper talk, and I had to admit that I wanted to now. I think I *needed* to.

Kai and I had recorded the missing segment about him and even the mention of the daughter I never birthed. That hurt like hell but I honored it – to my surprise, Kai's, and the others she'd brought with her. It was so odd having more young people in my house fussing about cameras, lights, and sound —she'd brought two helpers this time to speed up the process. It worked. They had good energy. Fresh life. Kai even stopped asking questions halfway through. She just let the camera run, and that's how she caught me at ease, telling stories and laughing nearly as much as I did in Key West with my friends.

When I saw her again to review the raw cut, she grinned and said, "I clipped that moment when you said you were afraid of being forgotten as a teaser on social media—hope that's okay. It already got dozens of reposts."

I kept my eyes on the screen. "Next time, check with me first, Kai."

"You're right. I'm sorry. It just felt powerful in the moment. I—I just...I was a little worried that I was trying to save a story I didn't have the right to touch and ignored my gut to leave it alone when I shouldn't have."

"Exactly. That's why it matters who decides when to share this." The words were sharper than I'd ever taken with her. But this was *my* story.

The next time we reviewed the footage an email pinged from a festival that made her eyes light up before she even told me what it was. She'd submitted the short.

Without confirming my yes.

"You're the heart of this thing," she enthused. "They needed a submission cut by today. I didn't want us to miss the deadline. I know. I know. I know. I should have gotten consent, first. Please don't be mad at me, Doc B."

"We talked about this!" I felt violated. Yes, I wanted to tell my story but not without full control. "You had time to ask, Kai. You literally ask a million questions about everything else." I got up. I didn't trust myself to sit still.

Kai looked at her feet. "I'm sorry. You're right."

"The segment was still raw. I hadn't decided if I'd said too much or too little."

She swallowed. "I didn't mean to cross a line."

"But you did. I appreciate you doing this, but this isn't your life on the line. You don't know a thing about what it costs to get here."

A long pause.

"I can pull it," she offered.

Was I really this mad or was I afraid? I wondered. "Argh, Kai!" I huffed.

"Want me to?" she asked sheepishly.

The room suddenly felt narrow and small. Part of me wanted to say yes, let it ride and just go for it. But this wasn't the book. This wasn't the page. This was my face, voice, and hardest truth submitted for strangers to judge on big screens in dark rooms. And I hadn't been the one to choose that.

"I need to think," I told her. "You really shouldn't have put me in this position."

"I apologize." She deflated, and I felt that too. *Sigh.*

Kai quietly packed her things and left while I sorted through my feelings. This was happening. Already, my story was no longer mine, but wasn't that bound to happen anyway? With the book? I'd have to promote it. I'd have to get in front of people whether online or in a bookstore to talk about everything. I couldn't hide behind the pen, paper, and laptop—not if I wanted all of this to mean something. Not if it was about legacy rather than vanity. The clarity made me feel exposed, but also accountable. I needed to talk to my friends.

THE NEXT EVENING, I was at Seble's condo. We sat on her wide balcony surrounded by potted herbs and lanterns, and the sunset dyed the sky apricot behind us. The breeze lifted just enough to make the sheer curtains at the door billow. Almaz brought a henna kit wrapped in patterned cloth, declaring, "I thought we should mark something tonight—maybe each other, maybe the moment." All of us wore bright colors and headwraps today. Unplanned.

The gesture made me smile wide. Almaz was such a walking embodiment of beauty and art. Yemi followed behind her with a small jar of homemade spiced honey and told us it was, "For the tart I brought... and whatever else needs sweetening."

And me, I brought the truth. After the situation with Kai and everything else weighing on me, I knew I needed my friends' input to help me sort everything out and make the best decisions. We first shared desserts, then stories, before putting our heads together to talk solutions. We did this while easing into what Almaz had called "the art part of the evening." She'd already unrolled the henna cones and was swirling lazy vines along Yemi's wrist while I continued chatting.

"It is hard for me to be mad at Kai and proud of what she made at the same time," I confessed, watching the paste darken as it dried on Yemi's skin. Then I told them about my book progress, and how excited I was about publishing— also with Kai's help.

"You're next," Almaz nodded towards me as if she didn't hear me, but she did.

I extended my hand. There was something grounding about the cool substance against my pulse points. As Almaz painted, Seble exhaled like she wanted to say something stern but chose not to. Yemi dabbed a bit of spiced honey onto a wooden spoon and held it out for me to taste it.

"Bittersweet," I noted.

"Precisely," she responded. "Look, Makeda, the child was out of order, but you will be seen. That's the part that matters."

I held her gaze. "It's also the part that terrifies me."

"Think of it as her pushing you, not betraying you. Besides, you didn't tell her to pull it."

"Mm hm," I murmured. What started as Kai's school project clearly turned into something neither of us expected. Somewhere between interviews and memory fragments, it became a living record. Not just of me—but of what silence costs. And...much as I hated to admit it. My friends were right. I needed the reckless push Kai gave. "Fine," was all I could push out.

We sat quietly for a moment, letting the sounds of the city rise to meet us. Distant horns. A yappy Pomeranian barking three floors down. Someone playing an old Aretha Franklin track from a nearby apartment.

Then without explanation, I blurted, "I also heard from Alex."

"Who?" They asked in unison. It had been years since I mentioned his name to them. Many years.

I refreshed their memories and instantaneously, the art

party halted. Almaz stretched her limbs. Seble set down her glass. Yemi tilted her head. I caught them up on that too—even showing them the old childhood photo I recently saw of him and recent images of him that I found online. I told them that just before our Key West trip, I'd run into him while picking up my medication and he, again, extended a flimsy olive branch. But I didn't want him ruining my plans.

"What will you do?" Yemi asked.

"Yes, what now?" Almaz piggybacked.

"Now...honestly, I'm tired of wondering what might happen if I don't try to meet him halfway. After all, he did take the first step."

"After abandoning you," Seble scoffed.

I didn't take the bait. I pulled out my phone, scrolling to his contact as if on autopilot. My knee bounced involuntarily from a sudden rush of nerves. It was as if I were outside myself.

Almaz leaned forward. "What are you doing?"

I said nothing.

"Makeda?" They pressed.

I nodded, feeling possessed. "Calling him. Right now."

A collective gasp. I stepped inside, out of earshot but visible through the sliding glass door. I tapped his name, and it rang once. Then twice.

"Mother?"

I swallowed, steadied my breath. "It's me."

Silence.

"Yeah, now...uh, now's not really a good time." He didn't sound good.

"What's going on? Where have you been? I think it's time we sit down and talk."

"I—I can't right now, I'm sorry—"

"But it was your idea, Alex," I gulped.

"I know. I realize that. It's just...I didn't think you'd *actually* call," he sniffled.

"Son?" My gut was screaming that something was wrong. "Are you alright?" My friends looked inside as if I were a rare animal exhibit. I paced.

There was a long pause. Then, barely audible: "She left."

My breath caught. *She.* I didn't need to know the name. I knew. The beauty from Opal & Vine. Her "yes," really was the *no* I suspected.

"And I got into a fight," he added. "A real one. Like...fists. Blood. Over nothing. Over everything."

I pressed my fingers to my forehead and temple.

"Where are you?" I found the nearest seat. My body was a jumble of emotions.

"Home. Back in Miami."

"Then see me."

More silence. "Moth—Mom..."

"SON."

A beat. "I don't look like myself right now."

"That makes two of us."

He exhaled with a tired laugh. A silence I refused to fill fell between us before he finally said, "Fine. There's a place —cheap, off Biscayne. I don't really want to run into anyone right now. Tomorrow at 11?"

"I'll be there."

Click.

Almaz didn't even pretend she hadn't been listening. "Do you want us nearby? We'll sit two tables over with sunglasses and attitude."

Yemi raised an eyebrow. "Or we can wait in the parking lot. Doors unlocked. Engine running."

Seble sipped her wine and didn't look at me when she said, "Don't let him waste your peace trying to find his." She sucked her teeth.

The air felt thick.

"I'm going," I responded. "No matter what version of him shows up. It was time I hear more than my half of our story."

20

THE DINER

I t was the kind of place you pass a hundred times and never notice. The "Open" sign stuttered in tired red neon, as if that were enough. Maybe it was. The air inside smelled like fryer oil and burnt coffee, nothing I would ever expect my son to indulge. I took a booth near the back and kept my rain jacket on. The table looked clean but felt sticky.

Alex walked in ten minutes late, hood over his head looking down at his wrinkled navy sweatpants. I almost stood up, but something compelled me to stay down. This was not the man from Opal & Vine. Not the immaculate man from the magazine. Not even the well-kept version from the pharmacy. His bottom lip was cracked at the left corner and his knuckles were darker than the rest of his hand. There was a swollen little knot near his temple, barely visible under the brim of his Marlins' baseball cap.

He gave a barely perceptible nod when he saw me and made his way back.

I didn't hug him. I wanted to but couldn't. *What happened to my child?*

Alex sat across from me and kept his sunglasses on.

"You came," I spoke first.

"You called," he replied.

We stared at the laminate menus between us. Unsure. Uncomfortable. If Yemi were here, she'd get on my case for letting pride overtake love.

"Your lip—does it need ice?" I asked him. "Are—are you hungry?"

He shrugged like a teenager. "I don't know."

Alex gently pulled his glasses off like it hurt. His eyes were bloodshot, either from a fight, alcohol, lack of sleep, or all three. I watched him trace a kidney-shaped water ring on the table with his index finger in the awkward moment.

"I don't know how to talk to you," he spoke again.

"Then start small. Say what you came here to say."

He finally looked *at* me. Not past me or through me. "Well, I came because you asked."

"Is that supposed to mean something? Because I *asked*? Like it wasn't originally you who reached back out because you were starting a family? Who didn't double-down on reconnecting that day at the pharmacy?" Tension. Already.

Alex winced. "Okay. Okay...um. I didn't say it right."

"No, you didn't."

A waitress appeared with a lazy greeting and, "You guys ready to order?"

"Not yet, sorry," Alex responded quickly while I shook my

head no. She gave a forced smile and walked off. The menus stayed closed between us while a sour silence filled the space. We didn't even need menus. Both of us needed to stop pretending that we didn't resent each other.

"I messed things up," he picked up again, anxiously tapping the table with his three middle fingers.

"You pulled away."

"You left first." His words were a forceful whisper—a wound. "Maybe not physically, but you weren't there!"

My throat tightened and my heartbeat high-jumped. He was clearly reaching decades back to the first cracks in our relationship. "I didn't leave. I was there, damn it! *You* stopped opening up to me. *You* stopped needing *me*."

The waitress passed by, leaving two glasses of water. We didn't touch them. Alex shook his head in dismay. "You stayed in the house, sure. But you left Pop behind and dragged me to Florida, then you emotionally left me to fend for myself. In that little room with your silence and your schedule and your goddamn grief."

I opened my mouth, then closed it. That last word hit harder than anything else.

"You gave more time to your rituals than me even before you and Dad split." Alex twitched.

"They kept me sane," I spoke honestly though the words were bitter. "When everything else felt like drowning in a foreign life."

His nostrils flared. "You were still married. You had me. You had a family."

"I had a role. One I couldn't breathe inside anymore no

matter how perfect it looked from the outside looking in. I'd outgrown it. I couldn't stand up in it."

"You couldn't breathe?!" he scoffed. "You had the house. The job. The lectures. You had *respect*. And if you and Pop could break up so easily, why couldn't you just stay together? Clearly, you didn't hate each other! I was the one suffocating. No one ever asked me if I wanted to move. If I wanted to start over."

"I'm sorry!" the apology jumped out without a parachute. It surprised us both. "You were a teenager," I caught myself. "What would you have said?"

"That I hated Miami. That I hated the new school and didn't know how to fit in with everything being so hard-times Black all the time—it was a different kind of vibe and energy than DC. At least there was an Ethiopian crew there. Pride, you know? Something. Miami wasn't nearly as..." he paused. "Dignified. Or diverse."

"What?"

"It's not that Miami was too Black. It's that I didn't know how to be Black like *that*. I didn't grow up with grills and fast slang and people calling me 'Africa' as a part of their ignorant jokes. 'Monkey boy with the blue eyes,' kind of stuff. I didn't know how to belong there. And... you weren't emotionally available to help me figure it out. I... missed you. And Pop. Our family."

I blinked. "You never said that."

"Because you were already mentally gone by then," he snapped. "You were unreachable and in this whole new world that I didn't really fit into. You had your books and your fucking candles and your little sayings in Amharic that made me feel like an outsider in my own house."

"Alex."

"I invited you to the parent showcase, remember that? Eighth grade. I was the only one whose mom didn't show. You had office hours. On a Saturday." He forced his eyes closed and I could feel his legs shaking under the table. "I waited for you. And when I got home you told me to grow up and stop needing applause for everything."

I didn't remember the moment he was talking about but could imagine my younger self responding like that. His pain crushed me. "I probably said that because I thought needing constant praise made you weak. But... I— I had no right to pass that on to you." I took a breath. "Your world wasn't mine. And... I'm sorry I didn't understand that in time."

Alex was mute. He barely moved. Nothing. He just stared at the table like it would give him back a piece of his childhood.

"Son, I didn't know you felt that way," I stretched out my hand with a tear sliding down my cheek.

"I guess I didn't know I did either," he finally muttered without meeting me halfway. "Not until just now."

I retracted. Defensive. "You know...I didn't even have any friends back then. I was alone too! I would go days without speaking to anyone who wasn't you—barely—a student or a syllabus. And...but wait... wait, wait, wait! Alex, the age you're talking about was *before* we even got to Miami! I thought it was Miami you hated! Or was it just—"

"There was another time after we got here." He overrode

my final word. "I waited for you at the senior debate finals. Told the two friends I had that you were just late. Watched every other parent walk through that auditorium door except mine. And when I got home, I told myself maybe you'd forgotten or mixed up the day—but deep down, I knew it wasn't that. You were just busy in your own pain again. After that, I figured out how to stop needing anything. At least from you."

I felt my face constrict in disbelief. *Had I really done that* **twice**? I didn't even remember the finals. Not a sliver. And he'd been on a stage, waiting for me. Expecting eyes scanning the room, hoping to lock onto mine. *Oh my God...*

He shook his head slowly, not with rage this time. Something else. "I learned that day how to go quiet. I didn't even know I was learning it, but I was. So...well, yeah... the disappearing thing...I pretty much learned that from you," he said. "If I was really in a bind, I'd call Pop. He was about as helpful as wallpaper, but at least he was available. I don't know, Mom. Maybe I just couldn't tell if it was Miami I hated or just the feeling that you weren't really with me in it. I really don't know."

And with that, I realized how badly I had failed him. How my survival looked like abandonment to someone too young to understand it. And how his silence had been both punishment and protection—his way of becoming me, and not becoming me, all at once.

Another couple entered the diner, sending the bell above the door into an annoying jingle. Someone behind the counter laughed too loudly. Meanwhile, neither of us turned.

We eventually ordered salads to placate the waitress but continued talking, barely touching the food.

Alex finally spoke again. A little softer now, less heavy from the load I'd made him carry. "Sometimes I couldn't tell if you were proud of me or embarrassed."

That pierced deeper than anything else so far. "What do you mean?"

He wet his lips. "You corrected how I talked. Pushed me to dress better, sit straighter. But you never really celebrated anything I did. Not in a way that felt like love."

"Not true! I was just trying to help you thrive."

"Maybe. But it made me feel like I wasn't enough. Not strong enough, Black enough, white enough, or even Ethiopian enough. Just one of your rough drafts you kept correcting but never published."

The words sliced like a machete, and my body flushed with searing regret. My eyes grew wider than I thought possible. *Oh my. My baby.* My body rocked with guilt. "That's not true. You were the one who wanted etiquette classes and wanted to 'talk properly,' hold your forks 'the right way—'"

"What's wrong with that—" He stopped before the last word could curl up into a question. Realization. "Well, I thought maybe if I got everything 'right,' I'd feel more like I fit somewhere." Alex erupted, sniffle and all. "That being proper would make me worthy of something to you. But all that did was make me feel like a knock-off with good posture."

Tears boiled and burned in the corners of my eyes. "I never said you weren't enough of anything for me."

He looked down and let out a breathless laugh. "Maybe

not. But it felt true." His snicker was part pain, part exhaustion… like he'd finally cracked the code of his own sadness.

"You were my world, son. You still are! I've missed you more than you could even know." The truth cascaded out. I gulped. My belly flamed.

A silence. We both exhaled. Alex picked up his fork and dropped it again. It looked like he started to reach for my hand but stopped short. I couldn't tell. I felt a bit of brain fog settling in or missing time. Damn it. Not now. I fought it back, as if I could overpower time and health itself. I *needed* to.

"I was figuring out who I was, Alex. I didn't mean to figure it out at your expense."

He tilted his head. "Do you really think that's all it was? Self-discovery?"

"I think I was trying to survive a version of motherhood and academia and everything else I fell into that slowly erased everything I'd once been."

"So, it was my fault?"

My mind stuttered. Static buzzed behind my eyes. *Had he already asked that?* I rapidly shook my head as if it would steel me in the present moment. I knew it was the stress and the disease gelling inside me at the worst time.

"No. You became my mirror," I whispered louder than I should have, suddenly more aware of the stale air and random people around. "And I didn't like what I saw. Not because of you. Because of how small I'd become. Alex…before I was your mother, I was a firebrand. Before I was your father's wife, I was Makeda the rebel. The activist. A woman people tried to silence in three languages. I was my own person with my own voice—loud even if unpolished, and unapologetic. I accidentally killed that part of me. Buried her so deep that I even let go of her true name to become 'Mae.' I had to blend to survive or risk becoming something exotic that people constantly wanted to examine or befriend for all the wrong reasons. What you don't understand is silence kept me alive longer than honesty would have in my new life, at least in the functional sense," I told him. "Hell of a trade-off," I then mumbled more to myself.

"Sure feels like I broke something in you just by being born," he mumbled, solely focused on himself.

"You didn't break me, baby, but clearly, I didn't know how to mother you without vanishing myself."

He pressed both hands to his face and sighed. "Then maybe you should have married an African man who would've let you stay Makeda."

"What?!" The words felt like a taser jolt. My mind flashed white, then black. Memories. Choices. I didn't answer him. I couldn't. Because I had no idea why he pivoted.

"And you could've just said that!" Alex continued. "You could've said *anything* instead of going quiet and letting the silence raise me!"

"What about you? You started telling people I was dead. Not 'out of your life.' Not gone. *Dead.* Do you know how that made me feel when I found that out?" I heaved in a breath. "So, you vanished because you thought you didn't need me, fine. I could've lived with that. But telling people I was dead was deliberate cruelty. And it shattered something in me that I don't even know can even be healed."

He gulped and blinked rapidly, like he'd never considered what the other end of unexpected death could feel like. "I was angry. And it was easier—."

A bitter laugh tumbled from my lips. I didn't try to restrain it. "Easier than saying you didn't understand me anymore?"

"Easier than admitting I was embarrassed and confused! By not knowing—"

"I can't believe you—" I cut him off.

"Let me finish, Mother!" There he went again with the *Mother,* like it was some kind of shield that accidentally fell from time to time but that he'd fight like hell to keep up in front of him. "Sometimes I wished you'd just disappeared. Like for real. Just to make it cleaner." He cringed but didn't take it back.

Something in me buckled. My throat felt like a stone had been suddenly lodged in it. I could barely breathe, and for a heavy second, I saw red.

"Oh, Alex!" I blew out a gusty breath, took a sip from my water, and glanced outside. Gray clouds eagerly spit fine rain. I bit my lips and furrowed my brows as various scenes played in my mind. Finally, I spoke again. "I saw you the night you proposed to your girlfriend. At Opal & Vine. I was there...you know this, of course, because you looked right at me. Right through me."

"Mom, mom, MOM!" He banged the table before raising his hands and I again, saw the bruised knuckles. He was full of rage.

"You looked right past me like I was a thin layer of dust. And what happened to your face? Who were you fighting over her? Why were you out of the country?" Questions and emotions were chaotically flying now.

"I didn't know what to do! And I wasn't fighting over her, I —" he immediately looked down. Ashamed. "I'm—" For a split second, I thought he might apologize. But it vanished when he instead said, "I don't want to talk about that, please."

"Alex."

"Mother!" His body twitched as though he'd kicked the air under the table.

"I don't need to know every detail. But if you put your hands on a woman, Alex, I—"

"God damn it, I said I don't want to talk about it! It was a mistake, okay! Never happening again. Now leave it alone! I feel shitty enough!" He slammed his fist on the table before glancing around, suddenly self-aware.

My God... Had I made him this way? Or had life done that on its own? I couldn't have raised someone who would...my mind wouldn't even let me finish the thought.

We sat in that for a long moment as one of the pendant lights above flickered. A family in a nearby booth argued about dessert. The world kept pulsing, oblivious. Laughter bounced. Plates clinked. Syrup dripped. A muted TV showed fans cheering for a silly sports game. Meanwhile, we sat in wreckage, choked by all the things we waited too late to say.

"I can't do this anymore. Not today. I can't talk anymore about any of this."

"So, what are you saying?" I questioned.

"I'm saying that...perhaps this was a good start, but I'm

not sure we are even remotely close to being fixed. I don't know how to be around you again but..." his voice trailed off.

Progress. Kind of. I nodded painfully. This still felt like being left, but it was a different kind of leaving. This one had a crack of light inside it.

"You don't have to know yet. Neither do I. This isn't just about you." I reached for him, but this time he did meet me halfway. Trembling, I let a few fingers touch the top of his hand. Skin. I had not experienced my son's skin in decades. He raised his wounded knuckle to rub the center of my palm. Connection.

Alex looked me in the eyes, looking near tears. I let him see how much this cost me and how much I still had left to give if we could walk along this broken road without tumbling into more self-pity on either side. He eased back slowly, pulling his hoodie back over his baseball cap and grabbed his sunglasses from the table. Alex left a $50 bill— like it would pay for more than the salads. Then he cracked his knuckles and grimaced, forgetting about the damage he'd done to himself while beating up on someone else.

"I'll call you, Mom," he told me, but his mouth twitched as if he didn't believe it. "I promise." The final words felt firmer.

He didn't reach out for a hug. No apology. Not even a goodbye. He just walked out, head down and into the light rain. As the door swung behind him, I saw his reflection in the glass. Alex was taller than the boy I raised, but clearly still haunted by him. I huffed.

"Thank you for coming," was all I could whisper to myself and the energy imprint he left behind.

And as I sat alone in the booth, with my appetite buried under history, I realized something simple and searing: the hardest part about estrangement wasn't the absence, it was the presence with no place to land. Though my heart felt a little bit at ease with the ownership of my feelings, I couldn't believe how my son and I had just sat across from each other like strangers with matching scars.

21

AFTERTASTE

It had been two days since the diner. Two days since Alex walked out into the downpour with hunched shoulders and no effort to look back. The talk left me wrung out, snuffing the thrill I'd been riding from my book, the film, and the rush of finally being seen. I wandered my apartment and shuffled books by color, then by author, then by how much comfort they gave me. I ignored calls from my friends but waited for one from Ezra. I lit incense without praying and walked room to room with a full laundry basket like a grief totem. I had no idea why I kept carrying it. Time stretched in all directions. There was so much of it and yet not enough to make anything feel in place.

Ezra knocked just after six. I appreciated that he hadn't used the bell. The last thing I needed was something that sounded like an intrusion rather than a welcomed arrival.

I opened the door barefoot, small traces of henna still on my brown skin.

"You look like you've been thinking too much," he offered a small bouquet of flowers from his backyard garden.

"Maybe I have," I smiled. "Come in." This man already relaxed me with his presence and unexpected gifts.

We sat on my balcony for a while, slightly baking in the late summer air. There was clingy humidity, but it didn't break into rain. A little wind here and there gave relief. I'd rather be outside in the elements than inside among walls.

As we caught up on everything once more, I told him everything about the diner. What Alex wore. What he said. What he didn't. Ezra nodded and tapped his knees the way men do when they're dodging emotional landmines.

"That must've been a lot."

"It was. It still is." I didn't expect or want him to give me any solutions, but something in me sagged when he didn't.

Ezra reached across and touched my hand. His thumb brushed my wrist. I let the soft song of my neighbor's wind-chime sing between us before speaking again.

"My body's changing again."

Ezra's hand paused and he turned to fully look at me. "What do you mean?"

"The tremors are stronger. I've been a bit foggier…. slower to find words, and quicker to forget where I was going." I glanced down. "I almost fell the other day." I didn't soften it though I wondered if I should have.

Ezra stretched his neck and leaned back in his chair. He looked out into the middle distance like the answer might be floating somewhere in the trees or just out of reach.

"I'm glad you're being honest," he responded.

That was it. Apparently, that was the kind of honesty that

cools hands. There was no *we'll handle this* or any *"we"* at all. It *was just registered and then set aside.*

Hmph. That was odd, but I let it stand. "I don't need fixing," I added. "Just talking."

"I know," he answered quickly.

We sat for another minute. Then he extended his legs. "Hey, Mae. I should probably get going soon. I've got an early call in the morning."

"Oh?" He hadn't mentioned work once before that. Never, actually, did he have to leave due to work. I noted it. "Of course."

He stood and kissed my forehead. Ezra held it there long enough for it to feel like it should mean a lot. When the door closed behind him, my apartment contracted back into itself. I think I did too but wasn't sure. Either way, I could do nothing—too exhausted. I went to bed.

I DIDN'T HEAR from Ezra the next day, though I'd quietly hoped to. As the morning stretched into late afternoon, I kept my phone face-down all morning, but by noon I was dressed and out for an afternoon walk. Candace had promised my edited manuscript back soon and I was excited about that. I still had my goals. I still had my self-imposed deadline. And I still had work to do to get my voice out there while I could.

Three days passed. Then four. By the fifth, Kai showed up at the Center with a lopsided grin and a reusable grocery bag slung over her shoulder.

"Please tell me you're not still mad at me," she began with big, goofy eyes framed by fresh braids dangling from her head.

I sighed. Her colorful presence did lift my spirit.

"I brought amends," she continued. Kai lifted the bag and pulled out diced mangoes, beef patties and cocoa bread.

"No, child. I'm not mad at you," I grinned.

She bounced on her toes. "Yes! Yesss, Doc B! Also, updates. We got in."

"In where?" In the middle of all my chaos, I did eventually tell her to go for it with the film, but it had fallen to the wayside between Alex and Ezra over the last week.

"The festival. We got selected for the Voices Section, which is better than the typical screen slot. It's for legacy stories. They even bumped us to the main day!"

I blinked. "Oh really?"

"Yup! I mean it's not the Oscars, but it matters." Kai was so proud. "You still okay with it?"

I needed this boost. "Yes, yes, I am. When is it?"

"In a few weeks. Perfect timing to follow-up after your book release – if we time it right, that is. Anyway, let's get ready for all of it! You'll need something to wear. And words. You and the other two people might be asked to speak." Kai spoke without taking a breath.

I laughed despite myself. "You want me to write a speech?"

"Oh, no, no, no, noooooo. That's too serious."

Whew.

"Just be ready to say a little something that feels right

with the viewing of slices of your life. Who do you hope to help? That's enough."

That might be too much, I thought, but held my tongue.

She unpacked the food while I poured us both a glass of water. We sat on the floor this time, just for a change of scenery. It felt good getting down on the cushions, I only hoped it wouldn't be a struggle getting off them. I asked her to replay the final cut. I didn't wish for more flattering angles or fewer silences this time. I just enjoyed my doing exactly what I said I was going to do while I had healthy time: not be silenced.

When it ended, Kai reached over and rested her hand briefly on mine. "Thank you for letting me witness you. And for forgiveness and grace. Taught me a lot."

"Thank you for not asking me to be anything else."

Later that night, Candace called. "Your manuscript is done," she said. "I left you margin notes in track changes and sent a second file with none. You'll want both."

"Thank you, Candace."

"No, Mae. Thank you. I meant what I said before. This book is more than good. It is urgent. You've got lightning in your hands. Do whatever it takes to make it real. And if you change your mind about getting an agent to go more tradi-tional, let me know. I've got a referral for you."

"Duly noted."

I didn't sleep right away after we hung up. I opened the manuscript and scrolled attentively. There was a lot of red, but also a lot of knowing that it all meant elevating my work to shine its best. Then, I saw her final margin note. "This is your full voice, Mae. Don't shrink it. Not now."

That's when I knew whatever happened next—screenings, signings, reviews, silences—I would meet it with my eyes open. I wasn't healed or whole, but I finally knew not to bury any parts of me that wanted to live. And while this wasn't the season to relax, I knew now that I'd earned the right to rest without guilt when the time finally came.

22

THE QUIET LAUNCH

It took twelve days of margin notes, back-and-forth emails with Candace, and several ugly tears shed alone while reading comments. But I finished. Finally. My manuscript was formatted, proofed twice on two different screens, and uploaded. The night I decided to hit "publish," I was surrounded by mismatched throw pillows, thirteen crossed-out Post-it notes clinging to my laptop, and women who refused to let me do it alone.

Seble brought me a new blouse to wear when I "go live" to talk about my book – even though I never said I would do any such thing. With what account? I didn't even use social media. Almaz dropped a matte-black drone on the kitchen table. Its hard plastic clattered as she synced it to her phone.

"What in the world?"

"We can use my Instagram! We are archiving the moment from every angle," she declared, eyes flicking between screens. "One day, your grandbabies will watch it in 4K!"

Instant regret. Her face scrunched as soon as the word left her mouth. My heart kicked once, then stuttered. I looked down. A small knot of grief and guilt had to be swallowed back all in one bite. Yemi, ever the quiet disruptor, opened a box of strawberry cheesecake and slid it between us. "To keep everything sweet," she proclaimed. "Now, let Makeda hit publish before you launch her into more legacy." Her smirk landed just right.

The grandbaby comment brought my unresolved relationship with Alex to the forefront. He had no children, but as my one and only, he *was* in the book. Whether he wanted to be or not, although I didn't name him outright. It was my story and not one of blame or revisionist pain. I told it straight and let the book sit with whatever that stirred.

"Makeda, write your name," Almaz interrupted my thoughts. "And the first line of the book that changed you."

I chuckled. "What is this, a publishing party or a séance?"

"Both!" she winked and turned on music.

When the time came, I clicked the button with bated breath. No one said anything in that single second. Then Seble exhaled and mumbled, "Well damn. It's real! You are a published author in the most personal sense. Congratulations!"

Almaz pressed record and asked, "How does it feel?"

I couldn't find a polished answer. "Like I just pressed my hand into wet cement." I beamed, completely okay with however it might dry.

Yemi whispered, "Then let it set, friend. Let it set." Her eyes held so much pride that for a moment, she felt like a mother to *me*. Oh, how I loved Yemi. She handed me a congratulations card on heavy stock that read: *Makeda Bekele. At last, in her own words.*

Before I could say another word, a call from reception came that I had a delivery. It was a short brown box of printed copies that I'd ordered separately to have for my first signing event. Thirty paperbacks. My name. My cover. My words, bound in ink. I held the top copy in both hands to feel its weight. It was perfect!

This was the afterglow. The truth was, I thought finishing would feel like fireworks but it landed like the last exhale after a long run. Good, even great, but quieter than I'd imagined.

The next morning I woke up electrified. Re-energized. I was primed for the book signing at Books & Books to come next—Yemi, who was friends with the events coordinator, had set it up for me. Purple and gold balloons were out front. A beautiful table with three neat stacks of my books, and even a bouquet of closed white lilies signed "In Charlotte for business but wanted to say congratulations. -A" were there that afternoon. Alex. Progress. I honestly hadn't expected anything from him.

The event was surreal. It also felt smaller than I'd dreamed, but I didn't say that out loud. Notably absent was Ezra, but I pressed on. The store staff were kind, though, offering me mint tea and letting me know they'd be just a few feet away if I needed anything.

Kai had arrived early, towing a wagon crammed with camera gear and enough lights to stage another short film. She wore combat boots, a cropped tee, and faux locs that made her look both ready for war and a glossy magazine shoot.

Seble gave her a once-over. "So, *this* is the curious filmmaker?"

Kai smiled without missing a beat. "Guilty and grateful."

Almaz grinned, already a fan. "Well, welcome to the auntie circuit!"

"I've been manifesting this moment! My mom is actually coming out tonight too."

That surprised me. I'd never met her mother. Kai must've talked about me more than I realized. She soon took footage of everything. The store entrance, the table, the flowers, my hands, the books, my friends and any stragglers, me with the staff. She interviewed Almaz and even Yemi.

Yemi laid out a table runner stitched with my name on it in a shimmery gold script. Seble fluffed my curls too much and insisted on a pair of earrings that felt heavy for how quiet the room was. "You want to look like the woman who wrote this," she said. "Not the woman who almost didn't."

I glanced toward the hallway but didn't see anyone else coming. Almaz and Kai fussed over photo ops and angles. This was really happening! The first guest arrived seven minutes early. She was there for a different author's event but wandered in anyway. A couple who also met regularly at the Center showed up. They waved kindly and asked for two signed copies, which swelled my heart with pride. Kai's mom also swung by. Just long enough to thank me for being part of the project. That felt like a gift.

Ezra arrived right as I started reading a short passage

from *How to Stand in a Room Without Disappearing—a piece about posture, voice, and what it means to take up space when history has trained you not to.* The pulse in my throat picked up when his blazer entered the corner of my vision. He wore a blazer over a T-shirt like he wasn't sure how dressed up this was supposed to be. When I finished reading, Ezra walked up and kissed my cheek. He smelled like laundry. I stiffened, trying to hold my jumble of emotions inside for the moment.

"I'm proud of you, Mae." He presented me with a wild bouquet of coral peonies and eucalyptus, setting them right next to Alex's, though his did not come with a note. Then, he stepped back like a guest at someone's wedding. Ezra watched the rest from a distance, and at some point, slipped out before the final round of applause.

My heart cracked, but I didn't go looking. He was exactly who he claimed not to be. Besides, I didn't write this book to impress or keep anyone. I wrote it to stop disappearing. To stop making space for everyone but me.

The first time I lied to America, I mourned the living, then let the world believe I was harmless, obedient, quiet. The last time—in this moment—I mourned the woman who made herself small to survive all that. That woman might've followed Ezra out the door. She might've even pretended it didn't matter just to keep him close. But I didn't. I wouldn't. I already missed her and pitied her. Forgave her, too. She kept me alive. But she could rest now, knowing this book was her truth, and it was out there in ways she never could be.

Outside of my friends, I signed six books. One was for a woman who thought I was someone else but still walked away with mine. That meant more than I could say. Another was for the barista who snuck away from the café counter for five minutes just to say she'd heard me talking once and that I had "an author voice."

When things wound down, I tucked Alex's note into my pocket and helped Kai collapse the tripod. She paused and locked eyes with me with that too-focused gaze of hers.

"This can't be it, Doc B. You've got something amazing here. We just need to push it harder."

Almaz was already nodding and agreeing. How did I not know these two would get along great, forty-five years between them or not? "We didn't film all this for archives. Let's edit some of these into reels tonight! I might have contacts to reach some legacy media, too. Let's go!" Almaz added.

Seble gave them both a look, then shook her head. "These two might be a dangerous combination. What are you even talking about?"

"Content," Kai said, stripping the lens from her camera. "Story clips. The reading. Voice pops for social media. I *know* people will care about this story. We just need to let them know it exists."

Almaz grinned. "I'll post the behind-the-scenes first. Make it look intimate and iconic. Besides..." she paused to collect her thoughts. "We've already had a mini viral moment – remember the Key West shoot and the girls who tagged us? That took off because one of them ended up having a podcast or something. Why not reach back out?"

That was a great idea! Chills. I started feeling them as we

stood there in the soft close of the bookstore lights—me, Almaz, Kai, Yemi, and Seble still pretending she wasn't smiling—and I realized this wasn't an ending. Not even close. I'd shown up. Now we were about to show out.

23

BEFORE I AM ERASED

T he buzz began the day after the book signing. Or rather, *it gathered* over the next two weeks. Every-thing came together like a low-pressure weather system pulling attention instead of rain. Kai stayed up past 3 a.m., editing with the kind of tunnel vision only youth and obsession can fuel. By sunrise, she'd sent us a Dropbox folder labeled: *"Doc B - The Becoming."*

Inside were five video files: sharp cuts, soft pans, grainy glimpses that felt more honest than any memoir. She included footage from the signing. Shots of the reading table, strategic footage of the few people I'd engaged, the glint of wine in paper cups. Ambient clips of the Center—ceiling fans spinning like slow applause. And one reel that split the air like a match strike: "To survive, I shrank. But to live, I had to risk being seen." You could hear the crackle of traffic leaks from outside in the background.

There was no intro or setup. It opened mid-sentence, like

we'd all just walked in late to something private. Almaz uploaded it with one caption: "She's been holding this for decades. We're not letting it go quietly."

By Wednesday, someone on Threads posted the lightning bolt clip with the caption: "Why is no one talking about this revolutionary woman???" It picked up rapidly. From LinkedIn to Facebook and even BlueSky. A few journalists privately messaged Kai. A Caribbean studies prof shared it with their department listserv. The wave had started and it was moving!

We made the kind of calls that made people clear their throats, and reminded them, gently and not, who I had once been in their lives. We pulled strings still knotted to grant boards, reunion committees, and long-dead newsletters and half-alive nonprofits. Every opening mattered, even if it only had a pinhole of light. Yemi whispered it down the church grapevine and through WhatsApp groups like it was gospel. Seble wrote a press email so precise it could slice a ripe guava clean from the pit. That one got me on an AM radio show—yes, they still existed and hit the right audience.

The station was tucked behind a Haitian bakery and a dry cleaner that doubled as a money transfer station. And the studio was the size of a confession booth. Stale air. Dusty surfaces. The mic had a strip of duct tape holding the foam in place, but the soundboard still worked and we even got a few callers dialing in! They wanted to know about my experience in the refugee camp, how it *really* was once I'd made it to America, and how I decided on a career path that led me to such a unique PhD in forensic linguistics. Another wanted to know how I'd managed to find such a strong sisterhood so late in life. Also, would I ever go back to Ethiopia? There was so much to talk about.

"Thank you so much, Zora," I gushed to the host afterwards. "That was my first time ever being on the radio!" What a day, what a day!

I had to sit in the car a while before turning the key. My hands didn't stop shaking until I pressed the button to start the ignition. I felt like a teenager again. Zora had smiled warmly and said she'd be at the screening, too. Yes!

I spent the next morning folding laundry with one hand and scrolling reactions with the other—Almaz would be proud of me. People were talking. I wasn't sure how to feel about it yet, but it felt earned.

My body tingled as I saw the engagement on everything go up by the hour, body trembling from both the excitement and probably the Parkinson's that reminded me it was still an opponent. But I took more medicine and pushed through that.

We reached out to the women who'd photographed us in Key West—the ones who caught us mid-laughter and mid-reinvention on that turquoise Chevy Bel Air. One of them ran a podcast: *High Tides and Healing*. The other had a modest TikTok channel: *The Third Draft of Me*. They both posted the clip.

One caption simply said: "These women are a masterclass in becoming, not just nostalgia."

The other invited me on an Instagram livestream. I had no idea what I was doing, but I had a great time fumbling through. Hundreds of viewers popped in and out with encouragement and awe—with Almaz being the main cheer-

leader in the digital room. By Thursday my own fresh Instagram with four followers shot to four hundred, and a TikTok
clip from the livestream hit 20K views overnight. Enough for
someone to pay attention. A producer from the Miami-Dade
Fest reached out to Kai. Someone from the Friday lineup
dropped out. Would we consider filling the slot? I didn't
hesitate.

"Yes."

THE NEXT DAY, we arrived forty-five minutes early. Seble had
steamed the hem of my dress while Yemi helped clasp my
bracelet. "You only get one first impression," she said,
smoothing my shoulders like a mother sending a child off to
school.

"Yeah, yeah," I smiled and let them fuss. Truthfully, I
needed the care more than I realized.

The fabric nearly outshined the daylight, but under the
interior room's light, it glowed more like an ember. *Was I
ready to burn this bright?* My fingertips caressed the pendant
at my throat. The gesture comforted me in the absence of
something else my heart also quietly wanted. It prompted
me to inhale and exhale. To enjoy every second of this
moment.

The line soon curled around the building, and Seble
raised an eyebrow at the sight of it. "Well. I suppose dignity
can still trend."

Almaz was in canary-yellow silk donning a high headwrap that turned heads. Seble wore a column of ivory with

gold cuffs that caught the light each time she moved her wrist. Yemi wore regal teal—sophisticated, luxurious, radiant. Kai led the way in a burst of print and crisp sneakers with a backpack slung over her shoulders. And me? I wore coral. The same shade from the book cover. My hair was pinned in a crown, and around my neck hung the spiral gold pendant my mother had given me.

We entered the main screening room like a rumor the world was finally ready to believe. The air was electrified inside. Students. Journalists. Film buffs. Regular community folks. *Snatches of conversation hooked my ears: "That's the auntie crew from the beach reel!" "Wait, she wrote a book too?"*

A young woman in cat-eye glasses tapped her friend's arm. "I saw her on that podcast." My pulse jumped. They remembered me. Music and expectancy also filled the space. The room was alive. I felt a little sweat build at the base of my back. Despite all of our efforts, I wasn't sure if the crowd would be what we'd hoped. In fact, it was bigger.

"Is that her?"

"Yeah, I think she used to teach somewhere."

"I heard she worked with the cops or courts or something, too."

"Yo, she's low-key everywhere lately."

"She did both."

More pinches of conversation caught my ears as the convergence of my efforts to tell my story permeated the room. There were no flowers from Alex this time. None from Ezra either. Neither man was there, but it didn't matter. I WAS.

The lights dimmed, and the film started. The room stayed with it from start to finish, but the energy spiked during my segment. The final one. I wasn't sure what they expected from a woman like me. But they watched me share jagged edges from marrow to memory. They saw tears fall from the crease of my eyes and the pulse of my veins in tight shots of my hands. They witnessed Kai's relentless effort to help me tell my unfiltered story. All of them. And I stayed in my seat, letting them.

The reel unfolded like a prayer in motion—my voice, Kai's lens, and footage from six decades of living. My story. It ended on stillness. Me in a chair, looking into the camera without a fade or musical score. I stayed anchored in my seat, letting the whole room meet me for the first time.

Silence.

Then someone stood. Then everyone did. A standing ovation in South Florida. For me. At least, that's how *I* felt. The moderator stepped up as the credits rolled. "Please help me welcome the director and the three extraordinary women behind this story."

We stood together with the applause feeling strangely personal. It rang distant and deep in my ears like the ocean through a surf wall. It cradled me, and I floated in something older than language. And then questions came to resurface me. I stood taller than I ever had in my life.

Afterwards, we ventured to the rooftop bar for champagne. Kai had ventured off with her film friend on a high from the awards she'd won. With my friends, Seble insisted on clinking glasses before a single sip. Almaz refreshed the video page on her phone and whispered the number: "Three hundred and sixty-two thousand!" Yemi found a corner seat and just watched us with quiet satisfaction.

"You did it, Makeda," Seble said finally.

"No," I told them. "*We* did."

Almaz raised her glass. "To surviving."

Yemi: "To thriving."

Seble: "To refusing to vanish."

We drank. And for one impossible minute, I felt complete.

After the laughter and lights and late-night hugs, I found myself barefoot on my terrace. Coconut Grove blinked gently around me. My phone buzzed with a message. From someone I hadn't heard from in weeks: *I read the book. Heard about the film. It's hard, Mom. All of it. But...congratulations. You did what most of us only dream about. And I'm learning from you. –A.*

I wasn't waiting for acknowledgment in that moment. I was writing the next page, but I appreciated what he offered back. I knew for certain now that I could rest without him or anything else erasing me. And just then...another message dropped in from him:

PS: I'm sorry too.

My soul shook to life! Four syllables my heart ached to hear. So unexpected but so wanted and needed. "I'm sorry too." They echoed in my ear to create the most beautiful words I'd heard in decades.

24

AFTER I WAS SEEN

I returned home to find a flower delivery from Robert. The card read: *"Still cheering you on from the cheap seats, always."* I smiled. We may not have meant to be married forever, but we definitely had a lifetime friendship. Proof that relationships don't necessarily fail but are just a season that brands its color on leaves while still letting them fall. Besides, were it not for him, I would never know what the title "mother" felt like, even when it was heavier and confusing rather than celebrated.

The day after the film festival, I got a text from Ezra: *I was there, Mae. I watched from the back. You were radiant, as usual. But I didn't want to interrupt your moment. The more I sat there and watched how big you really were in heart and spirit, it hit me that maybe I was never the man to stand beside a woman like you —just lucky enough to be near you for a while.* The irony. I wanted to be mad, but on the heels of what Robert's flowers had meant to me. I found it hard to channel anger. I read

Ezra's message twice. It wasn't cruel or manipulative, it was just...

Another text tumbled in before I could finish my thought—he must have seen my read receipt. It read: *I'm really sorry for how I left things, Mae. If you ever want to talk, I'm here.* That part pushed me to give the response. But I fought the impulse to say, *I needed you when I was trembling. Not now.* Instead, I archived the message. He saw that I'd seen it. That was enough.

Days later, Kai forwarded a message from a known indie producer who wanted to option my book and consider developing a full-length film. I was shocked, and unsure what to do, so I sat with it for a while despite Kai calling and texting. I didn't ignore her, but I did say I needed a little time. Honestly, I didn't know what the best move was. Everything was happening so fast.

Kai was screaming and Almaz already eager to "figure it all out." The next day, a congratulations came from my editor, Candace. She still pushed me to go traditional, but I wondered why after having done so much on my own. Wasn't the point to own my story, not just the pages?

I needed time for all the dust to settle, but maybe I would consider it. As days turned into a week, I found myself touching the spine of my book and re-reading Candace's final margin note: *"This is your full voice, Mae. Don't shrink it."* Indeed. A few quiet days passed. I spent them rereading old journal pages and letting myself be still. Letting myself revel and enjoy.

I did hear from Alex again. We met at an Ethiopian café

called Tizita in Buena Vista to "catch up." He chose the spot, which pleasantly surprised me. By now, nearly a month had passed since my book release and film with Kai. Alex looked better. Much better. Sharp. Handsome. Perfect beard. Without bruises. He walked taller, though there was still a chip on his shoulder.

Outside on the patio, the air smelled faintly of charcoal and toasted spices—korarima, dried chilies, even a hint of ginger. But it didn't overwhelm. Somewhere inside, a woman laughed and the breeze carried warm hints of incense and something stewing. The café itself was narrow and ochre-colored, with green shutters faded from sun and salt. Its name was hand-painted in Amharic and English above the door, flanked by potted rosemary and a crooked bougainvillea that had begun to creep along the overhang. Woven baskets hung beside a small chalkboard menu.

Our conversation was less tense than the diner but not relaxed either. It was more like a negotiation where both parties forgot what they came to win. But we were trying. By the time our plates had been cleared, Alex was talking about the expansion of his hotel to Charlotte, and how it had to overcome several setbacks, but was finally moving along. He confessed that he'd considered moving there to fully see it through but was nervous about leaving anyone on his current team in charge of the Miami location. I nodded. I found it hard to fully pay attention the entire time.

Alex glanced past me, then froze. His entire body went tight. I followed his gaze to see two women walking on the sidewalk, mid-laughter. The shorter one wore a flowing halter dress in amber with leather sandals and a carefree straw bag. Her hair was a lovely soft twist-out. The other, slightly fairer, moved with alertness. She donned a cropped linen blouse tucked into a rust-colored wrap skirt. Her hand rested at the small of the shorter one's back—protective, subtle, unmistakable. I blinked. It was...her. And I recognized her first. Not instantly, but the laugh did it. Full, open-throated, and alive. Then, her...partner? And the way she clocked Alex the moment he noticed them. She stiffened. Eyebrows furrowed. Pulling the other closer. Then, she looked straight through Alex with eyes as hard as polished stone.

"Nyla..." the name slipped from his lips as he averted his eyes to the shorter woman. The lady he almost married. Alex looked like he was being suffocated. He gulped and crinkled his forehead in pain.

The women didn't break stride. Nyla finally looked over and noticed what had seized her partner's attention. She noticed him, and for a split second, her body stiffened like someone poked an old injury. But she didn't stop. Her gaze locked steadily on his before she turned back to her partner and walked on. Whatever control or dynamic he once summoned had no place here anymore.

Alex didn't speak. He reached for his water, realized it was empty, and put the glass back down. His knuckles pressed down against the wood. I could tell he wanted to say something but restrained himself. But I clocked the way his shoulders curled inward. Something in her presence deeply unraveled him.

"She looks happy," I said, gently. I wasn't sure I wanted to know what had passed between them. From the looks of it, it was for the better for her.

Alex stretched his jaw, and I heard the tension pop. Then, softer than I expected, he relented. "Yeah. She does."

We sat with that. There were no tantrums or questions. Just the sound of the street and two women disappearing down it, hand in hand.

BACK AT MY APARTMENT, I set my keys down and leaned against the door for a beat before locking it behind me. My shoes came off by the mat and my shoulders dropped. I moved slower now because I wanted to feel every step on the floor under me. Flashes of my lunch with Alex followed me – how he used to center every room he walked into, but not today. Not anymore.

I filled a glass of lemonade. I felt a brief muscle cramp in my neck, but thankfully it didn't compel me to sit down. I raised the glass and drank anyway. I was alone, but I could still feel my sister friends with me. With my book on the table where I'd left it, a pen beside it, and a folded note from Kai half-tucked underneath. I enjoyed the warm night and city lights that blinked across the skyline. And for the first time in a long time, I didn't ask myself how long I had. I asked who else I could still become.

25

(BONUS SCENE): THREE SHADOWS, ONE FLAME

WASHINGTON DC, 1993 | SUMMER

Breathe.

Slowly.

With closed eyes...

Inhale...Exhale...

Haaaaa....

I never told anyone about the woman who touched me like I was still here.

It was late. One of those D.C. nights that tingled under your skin. Wet pavement, horn blare, sweat in the collarbone. Summer heat. I'd wandered into a makeshift gallery bar in Shaw to chase noise. I needed sounds loud enough to drown out my lonely thoughts. It was the kind of place with warm wine, crooked art, and someone's cousin working the door in an Ankara headwrap and Air Maxes. Really, someone's brownstone turned hub for a night.

Me'Shell Ndegeocello played low from a small DJ booth

in the corner—*If That's Your Boyfriend (He Wasn't Last Night)*.
The sound was warped but the room was a full-on 90s vibe. I
had a paperback in one hand and my pager on vibrate in the
other, even though no one was trying to reach me. Holding
both made me look busy. Or maybe phantomly tethered. I
wasn't sure.

Freshly single and free of the wife title—and for the
weekend—of the mom title, too. I moved around aimlessly. I
was in my 40s then. Too old for nightclubs, but too young to
cry myself to sleep over a divorce that I initiated. Instead, I
told a friend I would meet her here, but at the last minute
she canceled. I went anyway to forget my life's shambles if
only for one night. Taking in colorful posters and chatty guys
in Karl Kani t-shirts, I offered a smile here. A head nod. A
rebuff of an advance there.

The longer I stayed, the more I could feel my edges again.
And as the music switched to *Outstanding* by the Gap Band to
Gogo classics like Junkyard Band's *Sardines*, my breath settled
lower in my chest. My spine remembered how to sway. My
eyes blinked slower. And the wine warmed my blood.

"Mae? I almost didn't recognize you!" a woman behind
the bar yelled with a bright smile. I could still remember her
heavy brass earrings to this day. They shone like the sun,
catching light with every turn of her head in the smoky
room.

"Life changes do that to a face," I said truthfully.

She giggled, but it wasn't dismissive. "No, you just look...
undone. But in a *good* way." She poured me another splash of
the warm merlot without asking. "Let the room see you right
tonight."

I chuckled, not having a comeback for that. *Maybe she's right*, I thought, making my way to a corner with my book. I needed time, though, so I sat back and let the room hold me while I tipsy-read God knows what—I can't remember what it was now.

That's when she appeared, walking like doubt had never dared touch her. Like she'd been beautiful too long to be surprised by it. Wide-legged linen trousers and a sleeveless green top that gleamed like wet clay, she easily stood out.

"Who brings a book to a party?" Her smile was lazy but her tone was velvet with teeth.

Nerdy me, of course, is what I thought, but not what I answered. Mild embarrassment flushed my face beneath a half-laugh, half-apology. I didn't know what to say.

She tilted her head without taking her eyes off me. "Is it worth interrupting?" She nodded at the cover.

I looked down, suddenly unsure of what possessed me to bring a novel to a gathering.

"Probably not," I finally spoke up.

"Shame. You look like someone who deserves a better story."

I slipped the manuscript back in my bag, brows furrowed. "Do you always start conversations this way?" I felt the liquor slip and slide through my veins. Gently playing with me.

"Only with people reading paperbacks in dim rooms like they're trying to disappear."

I hooted, sharper than I meant. "Well, is it working?"

She took a slow sip from her cup, eyes never leaving mine. "Not even a little." She sat next to me. Just enough so she didn't have to shout.

A silence in our conversation followed and an unruly yawn escaped me.

"Tired, eh?" Her accent was subtle—West African, but softened by time in the States. "Ama," she told me, offering no hand, just the name and a slight head nod.

"Mae."

"Mae?"

"Well, Makeda, but...most people call me Mae,"

"Which do you prefer?"

"Uh..." No one ever asked me that anymore. "Umm." I gulped. "Ma—Makeda would be nice tonight." It was a departure from whom I'd become through marriage and time.

"Alright. Easy. So, Makeda," she picked back up, "what are you trying to forget tonight?" Ama's body swayed to the music as she enjoyed her drink.

The question gave me pause. Who *was* this woman? "A version of myself I didn't want to keep, I guess."

"Good. Some versions don't deserve to be keened."

Intellectual, I noted.

Ama glanced toward the makeshift DJ booth, and around at each corner where laughter and conversation filled the horizon over the music. Me'shell Ndegeocello's voice engulfed the space again with *Soul searchin'*.

"Would you rather talk literature or men?" She piped up again.

I blinked. "Are those the only options?"

Before Ama could answer, someone quietly joined us. He was a few inches taller than her, with warm brown eyes and locs pulled into a loose knot. Something about him felt already familiar.

"This is Kojo," Ama introduced, touching his arm.

He nodded toward me with a carefree smile. "You're the one with the book," he chuckled.

"Apparently, that's my whole personality tonight."

Kojo grinned wider. "Could be worse."

"Oh?"

"You could be the one no one notices at all. But you're not."

Oh. I hadn't realized how invisible I'd started to feel until someone disagreed. Most of the time, when someone looked at me, they wanted to place me: professor, mother, wife, forensic linguist expert, woman-who-used-to-be. Kojo didn't ask or even stare at me. He just sat down and let Ama tangle her limbs in his. His eyes still tracked mine like they were listening, however, as he rocked and bopped to Guy's *Groove Me.*

Ama swirled what was left in her cup and stood.

"Come," she said, sort of like a museum docent beckoning someone toward a favorite piece. "There's a room upstairs. Cooler. Quiet. Less...obligatory. I'm sweating more than I'd like down here."

Kojo rose without a word. Fluid. Unhurried. Like he'd follow her to the edge of the world. I hesitated just long enough to feel it.

"It's just another part of the show," Ama comforted me. "But most people don't know it's open."

"Okay." I followed.

Forty-three, single, and more woman than wife now. My body had been waiting for this moment longer than I knew.

The narrow staircase smelled like Frankincense. It creaked under our weight. Even 20 years ago—the house was old. Kojo walked a few steps behind while Ama was at least three feet ahead. I had space. I could turn around. I could also leave. But I didn't. His presence was enough to feel the air warm behind me. Upstairs, the light changed. I didn't know where it was going, but I knew I wanted to follow it. I kept on, staying in the moment.

In this space, small lamps and standing fans opened up the room. Their hum barely masked the bass still thumping through the floor. But I had to admit, it was a reprieve from the noise, heat, and sweat.

The walls were lined with photographs—black-and-white portraits, mostly—Duke Ellington, Marian Anderson, Chuck Brown. And some unknown faces in mid-thought, women with hands pressed to glass, couples kissing.

"Kojo took these," Ama said. "Years ago."

"They feel...private," I observed. The alcohol I'd drank tapered off nicely, and I was fully aware of all the details around me.

"They were."

Kojo leaned in to adjust one of the frames.

"I was chasing stillness back then," he said. "Didn't find it often. But when I did, I kept it."

I stared at one woman in a headwrap and an open collar shirt, her mouth parted.

"This one is arresting," I murmured. "I love it. She looks like she was about to confess something, then swallowed it."

Ama smiled. "Maybe."

I hadn't planned to want anything that night. But want has its own calendar. And I was starting to feel like I wanted...I don't know. *Something.* Kojo stepped closer to the frame beside mine.

"What do you think that means?"

"Not sure.

"Could be mystery."

"Or protection," Ama chimed in.

"*You...*" he looked down and clasped his hands before speaking again. "Are drawn to the ones that hold back." He kept his eyes on the photo, not on me.

Ama moved behind me, close enough that I could feel her breath on my shoulder. "Or...maybe it means power," she added. Her fingers reached for the tag below the frame. They brushed the side of my hand. It wasn't an accident, but it wasn't urgent either. A test. I didn't move away though my heartbeat shifted gears. *Thump. Thump. Thump!*

Ama stood beside me now, silent. Her arm next to mine. Our shoulders almost touching. Kojo stayed where he was, a few feet behind us. Ama leaned in. Her hair brushed my arm.

"Is it alright if I touch you?" she questioned softly.

Oh my. Oh my. Oh my. Did I hear her right? Was it the alcohol again? The low throw of reverb through the floorboards? My imagination stretched towards something I shouldn't dare want. I turned to face her, Kojo in my peripheral now. He had the kind of face that made you look twice.

Sharp jaw, full mouth, eyes steady enough to quiet a room. And Ama, now looking at her dead on in good light. She had brown skin lit from within. Moisturized. Shimmering. Sweet-smelling. Cheekbones cut like intent, gold earrings and bare shoulders. Her presence was sculpted, but never still. And my pulse was in my throat. What struck me more than all of that was how still Kojo was. How he securely let Ama lead. Lead me to...wherever I was now that I wasn't sure if I want to stay or leave. *Stay.* I nodded affirmatively.

She smiled and placed one hand on my waist. The heat of it. The calm. Intoxicating without a tongue.

"I just want to see if you'll stay," her voice echoed my daring thoughts.

And I did.

Ama looked at my mouth. A silent request that I clocked. I didn't speak. I quieted my thoughts. I stepped closer. My breath and feet wavered, lips parted.

"You don't have to explain anything. Just feel it," Kojo whispered.

Ama licked her lips slowly and then...kissed me like it wasn't her first time. Her tongue was slight and barely grazed my bottom lip. There it goes. Threshold inebriation. My legs clenched and my eyes closed. It was tender enough to say she knew that it was *my* first time.

"Mmm" a low moan escaped me as Kojo stepped closer, a gentle hand on the small of my back. They surrounded me now, and I was heavy-breathing through open lips. Wanting. I remember thinking Alex might be expecting my call. Just to say goodnight like I always did when he was away on the weekends. But he was with friends. Fourteen, and lately indifferent to bedtime calls.

Or so I told myself.

I let the thought pass. Plus, I did not want to be *Mom* tonight. He would be fine.

Ama, Kojo and I didn't go far. Just past a hallway that smelled like clove, burnt sugar, and tobacco leaf. The room was narrow but curated. It was like a secret tucked into the ribs of the house.

"It's an old studio, but it's clean," Kojo assured me. The door was open just enough to tempt with permission. "A small bathroom right there," he pointed.

I ducked in for a quick rinse—face, underarms, thighs— just enough to feel like I should before something really got started. This time, they followed my lead. When we were done, the room was ready. Ama was a step behind me now. Inside, was a low cream-colored sofa sagged and standing fan that rotated slowly near the window. On the wall, a long mirror rimmed in string lights blinked. Someone had left a half-empty mug of something herbal near the turntable.

Kojo stepped out of his shoes and rolled his ankles once. Ama next, flexing her toes and walking barefoot across the rug like it was hers. And me, I leaned against the doorframe, sober enough to really acknowledge what I was doing here. Then I stepped fully inside. Fuck it. I wanted this.

As I treaded in, Ama's fingers slowly...certainly...trailed down my forearm, electrifying places that had felt forgotten for too long. Donny Hathaway's *I Love You More Than You'll Ever Know* murmured through the static.

"This song always wrecks me," I confessed, not knowing what else to say. The line gave me a place to rest my voice as I saw Kojo peel off his shirt.

With the saxophone and guitar winding its way into the room, Ama looked me up and down. "You are beautiful, Makeda. Your jawline..." she said as she ran her index finger across its outline. "Ethiopian?" she guessed at my ethnicity.

"Thank you. And nothing but," I smiled, instantly put at ease. "And you? Togolese—no," I caught myself. "Ghanaian."

"Correct," she beamed.

"And I'm just a yard boy," Kojo chuckled.

Anything but, I thought as I took in his body. He was lean where it mattered, dense where it counted. I watched him briefly cup and squeeze the back of his neck before releasing a breath.

Ama began undressing me now, reaching for the first button on my blouse. But she paused, holding my gaze. My heart rushed. Thighs quaked. Center pulsed. I touched her forearm and ran my hand up by the tips of my nails so she could feel a slight scratch from the journey. Instantly, the first button slipped free. She stopped waiting. Ama's fingers were warm. Outside, someone laughed—too loud and too far away to matter. The door stayed open. None of us moved to close it. I didn't want any of this to stop, not even for a second. And a blaze of the younger, bolder, dare-devil Makeda flashed in my mind's eye: The night could watch. I had nothing left to hide. At least not tonight. I wanted to be free of everything, especially what I was told I should be to be...good.

Sade's *Jezebel* crept into the room as I found myself sandwiched between kissing, grunts, moans, sweat, and pulse-thick wanting—Ama on one side, Kojo on the other. Hands roamed and meandered like domesticated serpents. Dangerous, but not enough to bite—unless I wanted them to. The smell of Ama's skin tasted like a luscious memory of freedom, and I fell into it heavy when I indulged in it.

From the center of the room to up against the wall, to the "bed" to the floor and even against a window, our fingerprints left deep indentations in time. I knew right then that I would *never* forget this night. The impressions glowed behind my knees and melted whatever instinct still said, "slow down." As Ama's lips explored my body and Kojo kissed and bit my neck. I could hear the shape of his breath —round, deliberate, like someone tracing circles behind my ear before sliding inside of me. The string lights in the mirror caught the curve of my back just long enough for me to see myself writhing and bending and ascending in pleasure.

"Oh my God..." I heard myself breathe in between hip thrusts, fiery lust, and kisses.

"Makeda...Ama...Kojo. Mmmm...Yes!" A collision of body and voices.

Round one: gasps, grinds, caught breaths.

Round two: sweat-slick laughter, teeth on skin, a possible voyeur.

Round three: staggered yeses, and then silence thick as honey.

And as we collapsed in the hush between heartbeats, one of Ama's curls brushed my clavicle. It tickled and then stayed there, the very permission we all finally gave ourselves to rest.

I WOKE JUST AFTER SIX. The smell of fresh coffee slinked through the door. My clothes were folded on the chair. Someone had draped a soft, thin blanket across the foot of the bed, but I didn't reach for it. I sat there for a moment, toes pressed into the rug, unsure if I was the same woman who walked in the night before. Not changed or reborn. Just... remembered. *Makeda.*

Ama glanced up from Kojo's shoulder, when I finally stood, her finger tracing the edge of his still-sleeping triceps. She didn't ask me to stay, but she didn't look away either.

"I should go before the city wakes," I said.

She offered a half-knowing smile and nodded once. "You already have."

I smirked, small and uneven. Then I stepped downstairs into the dim quiet, stitched with music still playing low then out into the humidity. I walked three blocks in silence before realizing I wasn't even headed home. With my pulse now in my shoes, I just wanted to feel the morning on my skin a little longer. I didn't tell anyone where I'd been. Not that week. Not that year. Not ever. But I remembered. Every time someone asked if I was ever reckless, I'd think of that night.

And lie.

THANK you for stepping through the hidden door! If you enjoyed this story, please leave an Amazon rating/review.

The next one belongs to Alex. His story begins "Hard to Hold." Start reading it here: *Hard to Hold The Keyhole Chronicles Book 3*

ALSO BY CHERIL N. CLARKE

ABOUT THE AUTHOR

Cheril N. Clarke is the author of nine novels, two stage plays, several short stories and poetry collections, and numerous children's books. She has been featured in *Curve* Magazine, *VoyageATL*, About.com, *Out IN Jersey*, *Burlington County Times*, as well as Phillyburbs.com, among others. Her creative writing website is CherilNClarke.com.

www.ingramcontent.com/pod-product-compliance
Lightning Source LLC
Chambersburg PA
CBHW050512260626
47157CB00004B/1293